Hot Brazilian Docs!

Sizzling Brazilian nights with the hottest docs in Latin America!

The hotshot docs of Santa Coração Hospital are all top-of-their-class surgeons—and Adam and Sebastian are no exception! But handling a medical emergency is nothing like falling for the two feisty, sexy women who stumble across their paths. Suddenly these Brazilian docs are further out of their depth than they've ever been before!

The **Hot Brazilian Docs!** duet
by Tina Beckett
is available from September 2017

Adam's story:
The Doctor's Forbidden Temptation

Sebastian's story:
From Passion to Pregnancy

And if you missed them earlier:

Marcos's story:
To Play with Fire

Lucas's story:
The Dangers of Dating Dr Carvalho

Dear Reader,

Best friends! They're always there for you—even when the relationship is on shaky ground. Book Two of my Brazilian duet finds childhood friends Adam Cordeiro and Sebastian Texeira in a tight spot. Adam has married Sebastian's sister, leaving his buddy high and dry. And Sebastian's quick encounter with an acquaintance has unexpected consequences when that acquaintance is hired at Sebastian's hospital.

A few weeks later there's an added complication in the form of a pregnancy! Sebastian's rigid determination not to follow in his best friend's footsteps is tested to the max. But being with Sara is like nothing he has ever experienced. And now there's a baby involved…

Thank you for joining Sebastian and Sara as they dodge life's curveballs. And maybe—just maybe—this special couple will find that some pitches are meant to be caught. I hope you love reading about their journey as much as I loved writing about it.

Enjoy!

Love,

Tina Beckett

FROM PASSION
TO PREGNANCY

BY
TINA BECKETT

MILLS
BOON

® and TM are trademarks owned and used by the trademark owner
and/or its licensee. Trademarks marked with ® are registered with the
United Kingdom Patent Office and/or the Office for Harmonisation in
the Internal Market and in other countries.

Published in Great Britain 2017
By Mills & Boon, an imprint of HarperCollins*Publishers*
1 London Bridge Street, London, SE1 9GF

© 2017 Tina Beckett

ISBN: 978-0-263-06976-1

Our policy is to use papers that are natural, renewable and recyclable
products and made from wood grown in sustainable forests. The logging
and manufacturing processes conform to the legal environmental
regulations of the country of origin.

Printed and bound in Great Britain
by CPI Antony Rowe, Chippenham, Wiltshire

Three-times Golden Heart® finalist **Tina Beckett** learned to pack her suitcases almost before she learned to read. Born to a military family, she has lived in the United States, Puerto Rico, Portugal and Brazil. In addition to travelling Tina loves to cuddle with her pug, Alex, spend time with her family, and hit the trails on her horse. Learn more about Tina from her website, or 'friend' her on Facebook.

Books by Tina Beckett

Mills & Boon Medical Romance

Hot Latin Docs

Rafael's One-Night Bombshell

Christmas Miracles in Maternity

The Nurse's Christmas Gift

The Hollywood Hills Clinic

Winning Back His Doctor Bride

Hot Brazilian Docs!

To Play with Fire
The Dangers of Dating Dr Carvalho

Her Playboy's Secret
Hot Doc from Her Past
Playboy Doc's Mistletoe Kiss
A Daddy for Her Daughter

Visit the Author Profile page
at millsandboon.co.uk for more titles.

To my babies.
You may not be little anymore,
but you will always hold my heart in your hands!

Praise for
Tina Beckett

'The book had everything I want from a medical romance and so much more… Tina Beckett has shown that the world of romance mixed with the world of medicine can be just as hot, just as *wow* and just as addictive as any other form of romance read out there.'

—*Contemporary Romance Reviews* on
To Play with Fire

PROLOGUE

Two things came to mind as Sara Moreira stood behind the bride-to-be.

One: she was grateful her boyfriend hadn't waited until her wedding day to ghost her. Instead, he had left in the middle of the night. No response to her texts. No returned calls. He'd just disappeared into the ether.

And two: Dr. Sebastian Texeira looked as gorgeous in a tux as he did in a lab coat.

More than gorgeous. Even when he slid a finger behind his bow-tie and tugged as if his collar were ten times too tight. Something he'd done repeatedly during the wedding, looking none too happy with the proceedings.

Why was she even noticing that? Wasn't she supposed to be knee deep in her own woes, not worrying about someone else's problems?

Her tummy tightened as she took in the broad chest and narrow hips. Wow, evidently her devastation hadn't reached the more primal regions of her brain.

Dr. Texeira's glance shifted with shocking swiftness and—*yikes!*—caught her staring. The second time he'd done that. His mouth kicked up to one side, sending her errant stomach diving feet first into a dark pool.

What was wrong with her?

This was his sister's wedding, for heaven's sake. She needed to keep her eyes to herself.

Besides, this man was way out of her league. Even further than the guy she'd imagined herself in love with. The man she'd cried bitter tears over a month ago.

Or had that just been wounded pride?

"Up here, please?"

Sara's attention snapped back to the minister. He'd asked something and was staring right at her.

Céus. Was she supposed to be doing something? Straightening the bride's train? Vacuuming the red carpet that covered the dusty ground of her dad's ranch? Lying down and dying of embarrassment?

The last option was a definite possibility.

A sense of hysteria began building in her chest before Dr. Texeira snagged her gaze once more, lifting his right hand and waggling his little finger. The glitter of a diamond band appeared. What the…?

Oh…ring! She was supposed to give Natália the groom's ring.

But where was it? Her mind went blank in an instant.

A few giggles came from behind her. Oh, Lord, she couldn't believe this was happening.

The good doctor came over to her. "Here." He reached for the bouquet she held. Tied to one of the ribbons was the errant ring. With a few quick twists, he teased it free of the knot.

"Give me your hand," he murmured.

She jerked it back in a rush.

"I'm just going to give it to you."

"Oh." Feeling like a fool, she opened her hand, and the sizzle of cool fingers brushing across her palm made her suck down a couple of breaths. She handed the ring over to Natália as if it were coated with poison.

It might as well be.

She looked back across the aisle to where he had retreated.

Okay, the man was now watching her with open amusement. Her lower lip jutted slightly, then froze when his gaze dropped to her mouth.

Mini-frissons of heat overtook each of her limbs.

Was she getting heatstroke?

What had her father been thinking, inviting members of his cancer care team to have their wedding at the ranch?

Dr. Texeira had been part of that team. And Sara had spent the better part of last year at his hospital during her dad's treatment.

And now Antônio Moreira was well again. *Graças a Deus*. She could feel his presence in the small group of people seated behind the wedding party.

Once they'd left São Paulo and returned home, she'd never expected to see the hunky doctor again. But here he was. And her thoughts were not the kind she should be having at a friend's wedding.

He'd looked at her mouth. She was almost sure of it. Except when she gathered the courage to glance through her lashes, she found him staring straight ahead.

She'd imagined it.

Just like she'd imagined him leaning toward her and...

"You may now kiss the bride." The minister's proclamation whipped that thought from her head and sent it spinning away.

The pair at the front of the makeshift chapel turned toward each other, their happiness almost palpable as they came together for a long, long, *long*—she counted down the seconds—kiss that had her attention sliding back toward the best man.

She gulped.

Not her imagination. He was definitely looking at her. Then the bride and groom broke apart and swept down the aisle, leaving them behind. Dr. Texeira pivoted, his shiny black shoes unscathed by the red dust that covered every inch of the ranch. He held his right arm toward her.

Oh! She was supposed to go down with him.

She settled her hand in the crook of his arm, trying to calm her rattled nerves. "Nice wedding, huh?"

"Yes. *Great*."

Hmm, that word didn't ring true. In fact, she was pretty sure he was lying, which was odd considering the fact that it was his sister who had gotten married.

She frowned. "Is everything okay?"

"Hmm. I just see someone I'd rather avoid." He glanced down at her. "Mind cutting through that section of chairs on our way to the reception?"

Maybe he was ghosting someone too.

Without waiting for a response, he towed her between the rows of organza-draped seating to their right.

"I think we're supposed to be following the bride and groom."

"Humor me for a second. We'll get there." Only there wasn't a trace of humor in his voice.

Who exactly was he trying to evade? When they reached her dad's huge barn, which had been converted into a reception hall for the big event, she led him to one of the side entrances. The massive sliding door stood open, and a drape of gauzy fabric had been interwoven with twinkle lights, a slight breeze making them wink in and out like stars against the growing dusk. "We can sneak in this way, if you want."

"Perfect, thank you."

Thinking he was just going to abandon her there at

the door, she was shocked when he cupped her elbow and ducked through the curtains, eyeing their surroundings before moving toward the table set aside for the wedding party. The same frothy organza that graced the chairs and all the entrances had been tossed over it. Placed on a wooden platform lined with more tiny glimmering lights, Sara had to go up three steps to reach it. Natália and Adam were already seated. The bride glowed with happiness, while the groom gave Sebastian a pointed look. "I wondered if you were taking off before the toasts."

"No."

The answer was short and curt, and he cut around the table and went to Natália, whispering something in her ear. She gave a quick shrug and glanced out at the guests. "There was nothing I could do. They insisted."

When Sara peered out at the tables, which were filling with guests, she saw a lot of strangers, so Natália could have been talking about anyone.

Just then, a small group with stringed instruments began playing, a fiddler stepping forward to set up a lively melody that drowned out Sebastian's response. And, of course, there were only two more chairs at the table. One for Sebastian. And one for her. Right next to each other. There were even little printed cards with their names on them.

Unfortunately, those seats had been placed next to the groom, so she didn't even have the luxury of turning and engaging Natália in conversation for the entire evening.

Did it matter? It shouldn't.

She should just sit back and enjoy Sebastian's company.

Except he made her just a little nervous. Because he was a city man like her ex?

Big deal. It was one night. She'd survived much worse.

He sat down next to her, his arm brushing her bare shoulder as he did. A shiver went through her.

Yep. Nervous.

One of her dad's rugged ranch workers, looking out of place in formalwear, brought a tray with four champagne flutes. His hands gave him away. Gnarly with calluses he grinned at Sara as he moved down the table and handed her a glass. "You look great."

"So do you, Carlos."

He then turned to Sebastian, his tray outstretched. Sara was unable to suppress a smile when the doctor took the proffered drink with a frown.

"You don't like champagne?" she asked after Carlos move away.

"I was hoping for something a whole lot stronger."

He had to lean close to make himself heard, and his shoulder bumped hers again. This time she went with it, not even attempting to put any distance between them. Instead, she focused on that point of contact and allowed herself a tiny forbidden thrill. He'd never know.

"Something stronger? At a wedding?"

"Especially at a wedding." The wry humor behind those words came through loud and clear.

"Drink enough of that stuff and it will probably have the same effect."

"So would cough syrup."

This time she laughed. "Okay, so champagne really isn't your thing. If you want something fast and to the point, you can always head to the Casa de Cachaça afterwards. I can show you where it's at."

Why had she said that? Maybe because he was so obviously unhappy about someone in attendance. And his "especially at a wedding" comment resonated with her.

Boy, did it ever.

At least her ex hadn't shown up tonight.

She scanned the guests again. Maybe Sebastian had an ex who had. Could that have been what he and Natália had been discussing a few minutes ago?

"*Cachaça* sounds like a good choice." Sebastian set his fancy flute beside the plate. "In that case, I'd better hold off on those so I can drive us there."

Us? An even bigger and more forbidden thrill cut through her belly. Well, she *had* just offered to show him where it was. He must have taken that to mean that she would be drinking with him.

If she was going to correct him, now was the time. Instead, she set her own glass down next to his.

Didn't she deserve to drown her sorrows? She had always been about playing the good girl, and look where that had gotten her: abandoned and forgotten. Couldn't she, for one night, do something daring? Something a little out of character?

She didn't have to work in the morning. And if she was honest, having a man like Sebastian take an interest in her was highly flattering.

Not that he had. Not really.

The sound of spoons clinking against glasses began to filter up to their table, growing in volume until it almost drowned out the music. Right on cue, Natália and Adam turned to each other and kissed. Murmured to each other.

She glanced at Sebastian. Not even a hint at a smile. Wow, something really was wrong.

Just then an older gentleman at one of the center tables stood and lifted his glass high, sweeping it from side to side as if trying to gain everyone's attention. The music stuttered, then faded to nothing.

The guest gave a toothy grin, staring up at them. "I'd like choo propose a toast. To my darrrrling girl and her new husband."

The voice slurred its way through the words, and the woman next to him tugged on his sleeve, urging him to sit down. Sebastian's hands curled into fists on the table, and he turned to Adam and Natália. Her friend seemed frozen in time.

"Do you want me to ask him to leave?"

Adam nodded at him, but Natália laid a hand on his arm. "No. It's okay. Mom will get him back under control. If she can't…"

The groom leaned over and kissed her cheek. "Just say the word, and I'll take care of it." He then glanced at Sebastian. "Can you propose your toast now, to get everyone pointed in the right direction? Then we'll get the dancing started. Hopefully that will circumvent any more problems."

"Sure thing." Picking up his own glass, he made a tall and imposing figure as he went to stand behind Adam and Natália's chairs. "Can I have everyone's attention, please?"

The whole barn went silent. He waited a second or two longer, and Sara was pretty sure he leveled a glare at the man who'd made the previous toast.

"I've known these two people for a very long time." A couple of chuckles came from the tables below. "And while in all those years I never dreamed this would happen, I'm happy for them. Genuinely happy."

His gaze softened, and he put a hand on Natália's

shoulder. Tears gathered in her eyes as she mouthed, "Thank you."

Sebastian continued. "And while I gave them a hard time of it for a while, I can't think of two people more deserving of happiness. May you have many years of it." He raised his glass. "To my sister and my best friend. Cheers."

Sara remembered to grab her champagne just in time to take a sip along with everyone else. Adam stood, and he and Sebastian embraced.

Then the groom held out his hand to Natália. "Dance with me."

They made their way down to the floor where thick wooden planks had been fitted together to form a dance area. The music started back up, taking on a slower, more intimate tone that was perfect for the couple's first journey around the room. Adam swept his new bride into his arms and smiled down at her.

It was beautiful. *They* were beautiful.

Her dad had made the right decision in having the wedding here, despite her earlier reservations. Sebastian sat back down, and only then did she realize he'd never lifted his glass to his mouth after giving his toast. Had he not meant what he'd said?

Struggling to find something to say, she settled for, "Nice job."

He gave that wry smile that jerked at her tummy muscles. "Would you believe I wrote the words on my palm so I wouldn't forget them?"

"No."

She'd seen those hands, and there was nothing on them except a light, masculine dusting of hair. Neither had there been anything on them when his fingers had brushed her palm in a way that had shattered her composure.

His smile widened. "Well, I probably should have. I think that concludes my duties as best man. I am more than ready for that *cachaça*. Do you want to stay for the rest of the reception?"

She had a feeling his real motivation in wanting to leave was to avoid the toast maker from a few minutes ago. The same man he'd been trying to evade earlier? It had to be his father. Or stepfather, if she was reading the signs correctly.

Did she want to stay? He was obviously giving her an out.

She should take it and run.

And do what? Sit here all by herself while the happy couple—and everyone else—celebrated all around her?

No. She deserved a little bit of fun too, especially after all she had been through in the last several weeks.

"I'm not really interested in staying. Besides, I need to show you where the place is, remember?"

He studied her for a minute. "Are you sure? I probably won't be in any condition to drive you home afterward."

"Don't worry about me. I'm a big girl, and this is a very small town."

"Let me tell Adam I'm leaving, then. I'll be back in a minute."

She had a feeling he wanted to make sure his friend could handle things with the older man, if they got out of hand.

A minute later, he was back beside her chair. "Okay, he cut me loose."

They ducked out of the same entrance they'd come in at. By now, it was dark, the lights from the barn spilling out onto the ground. When they reached the parking area, he stopped in front of a sleek silver sports car.

"Are you sure you want to ride with me?"

There was something loaded about that question. The memory of his shoulder pressed tight against hers rolled through her mind, along with a warm, prickly sense of need.

This was a man who could help her forget the ache of loss in a way that no amount of champagne or Brazil's famed sugarcane alcohol, *cachaça,* ever could. If she dared to let him.

And suddenly she realized that's exactly what she wanted. To forget. For a few hours. Or an entire night. Whichever one he was offering.

"I'm very sure. I'll ride with you."

He paused for a second, then leaned down and brushed his lips across hers, the briefest of touches that left her trembling and wanting more. So much more.

When he opened the passenger side door, he murmured, "Buckle up, Sara, because if I'm reading this correctly, things could get very, very bumpy before the night is over."

She sank into the plush leather seat and clicked her seat belt into place, yanking it tight. "Is that a promise?"

"It is now." His fingers feathered across her cheek and were gone. "And I never go back on my word."

It was all a blur.

Sebastian Texeira's arm stretched to the side and found…nothing. Sitting up, he scrubbed his fingers through his hair and glanced at the pillow on the bed next to him.

She was gone. Not even the indentation of her head remained. Should he be relieved or upset?

He wasn't sure of anything right now.

Deep purple curtains hid the view outside. And the same gaudy color was splashed with a generous hand throughout the room.

Damn. A motel.

But it had been the closest place to the bar. Not an accident, obviously.

He groaned and fell back against his own pillow. He hadn't even had the decency to take her to a respectable place?

The motels in his country were all used for the same thing. Cheap encounters at a cheap price. Normally the place where affairs took place.

The type of place his dad would have holed up for a few hours.

His father had been the reason he'd been hell bent on getting away from the wedding as soon as possible. He'd had no desire to talk to his parents. And that toast his dad had given had been cringe-worthy.

What he hadn't expected was for Sara Moreira to offer to go with him. Or to climb into the taxi beside him as he'd headed for this place. Which meant his car was still at the liquor joint.

He swallowed and closed his eyes. Except as soon as he did, images of the frantic press of mouths and bodies moving deep into the night flashed behind his eyelids. He snapped them back open.

He lifted the purple bedspread and peered underneath. Still naked. Damn.

Where were his clothes? He scanned the room.

There. On the dresser. His formalwear was neatly stacked and folded.

Relief was beginning to outweigh regret and the throbbing in his head. It was easier this way. She obviously didn't want to be found here with him. And that was fine with him. He'd rather her dad not find out about this at all. Although Antônio Moreira was no longer his patient, it could still prove to be awkward.

Climbing out of bed and stalking toward the bathroom, he showered quickly, using the tiny bottles of products he found on the counter. They were untouched, the seals intact until he opened them. She'd left in a hurry, evidently.

He finished and toweled off, his nerves beginning to settle as he padded back into the bedroom.

It was okay. Yes, he'd had a few too many drinks. Yes, he'd shared a couple of hours at a motel with a beautiful woman.

That this was not his normal behavior didn't matter. What was done was done.

The shock of his sister and his best friend deciding they were "in love" had still not worn off, almost a year later. He'd kept thinking it was just a phase, that they would get over it. They hadn't. And as of yesterday they'd sealed the deal. They were married.

He shook off the thoughts, snagging his clothes from the dresser and jerking them on. He should have at least thought to bring along some jeans to change into.

Grabbing his wallet from the heart-shaped nightstand, his lip curled in disgust at the gaudy furnishings, an over-the-top nod to what the room was designed for, from the cheerful wicker basket of condoms on the dresser to the...

His gaze jerked back.

Condoms.

And three torn Cellophane wrappers.

He blew out a breath. At least they'd been protected. Both he and Sara were free and clear. And that's the way he intended to keep it.

No weddings or rings in his future—he was strictly

a best man kind of guy. Although as he'd held that ring over Sara's hand, he'd had the weirdest sense of déjà vu. Only here in the motel room, there was no 'déjà' and no 'vu'. There was only him.

No wife. No children.

And "for as long as he alone shall live", that was exactly the way it was going to stay.

CHAPTER ONE

Four weeks later

"WE'VE FINALLY HAD someone respond to our request for a nurse. It looks like your mobile screening unit is a go after all. We still need to discuss the start-up costs, though."

The slums of Brazil weren't the most desirable place to work, and yet Sebastian had hoped for more than just one taker so he could choose the most qualified individual. Especially since the memo had been sent out to hospitals in various states of the country.

He sat back in the chair and regarded Paulo Celeste, the hospital administrator. "The costs are all listed in the dossier. I know we have a couple of ambulances that are out of commission. If we could use one of those, it would cut costs tremendously. I'm donating my time, of course, so that will help as well."

His trip to *gaúcho* country had brought more than just a wedding and a night in a motel, it had once again emphasized the need for screening services in areas where medical facilities were few and far between. Even in the state of São Paulo, there were rural locations that were difficult to access. And then there were the *favelas*. Hospital Santa Coração had a clinic in the slum down the hill, which was run by Lucas Carvalho. But if the mobile unit was up and running, they could go into some of the other areas as well.

The hospital administrator opened a folder on his desk. "So basically a portable ultrasound machine and some blood draw equipment?" The man peered a little closer. "And, of course, the nurse. She is willing to settle for the stipend listed as long as we provide her with lodging. Check and make sure there's a place available in the hospital housing division."

"Okay. And if there's not?"

The administrator made a sound in his throat. "We can't afford to rent her an apartment in the city." He shuffled through a stack of files on the right-hand side of his desk. "She's from a little hospital in Rio Grande do Sul. No local relatives. Her father was a patient here a while back, and she's anxious to do an *estágio* in oncology. With the hiring freeze it's a little tricky...but if there are no units in the hospital you could always consider housing her yourself." The man gave him a sly smile.

"I don't think so." That was all he needed. He'd just hope there was something available. "The hospital bigwigs would probably frown on that kind of arrangement."

"I *am* the bigwig, but yes. It was a joke. Professionalism is the key, especially in this kind of situation."

"Of course."

Wait. He flipped through his own mental file drawer. Rio Grande do Sul—wasn't that where his sister's wedding had taken place a month ago?

"Who was the patient?"

"I'd have to check. The daughter's name is Sara Moreira."

A stream of shock zipped up his spine. He knew exactly who that was.

Tall with legs that wouldn't quit, and expressive eyes that reflected every single second…

Deus, it couldn't be.

She was applying for the job?

"Does she know who the request came from?"

Paulo's head tilted. "It came from Marcos Pinheiro, since he's the head of oncology. Why?"

What was he supposed to say? "Oh, remember that whole *professionalism is key* thing? It's already gone way beyond that."

And boy had it. Several times. In multiple positions.

He swallowed hard. That was probably the dumbest move he'd ever made. And if he admitted to it here and now, his project was dead in the water. She hadn't been a nurse at his hospital at the time, so there had been no problem. Right?

When Paulo started to hand him the file, he waved it away. "I know who she is."

He wanted to tell the man, hell, no, he didn't want her. Standing next to her at that wedding had made something in his gut churn to life, just like when he'd worked her father's case. After a few drinks, things had gotten out of hand, and the rest was history. A crazy sensual history he was better off forgetting.

But if he said he wasn't willing to accept this particular nurse, he would have to explain why, and that could make for a very awkward conversation. It could also mean the death knell for this project, since no one else had responded to their request. Was he looking a gift horse in the mouth here?

He'd certainly enjoyed kissing that mouth.

He took a deep breath, hoping he wasn't making a huge mistake. "I can give her a try and see if she works out."

The administrator shook his head. "We'd need to be

able to offer her three months, minimum, and six months is what she prefers. She wants the experience, Sebastian. She can't get it in less time than that. Take it or leave it."

In other words, his pet project was resting on the answer to this one question.

The question was could he keep his hands to himself for that long? Yes. Some mistakes did not bear repeating, no matter how pleasurable they had been at the time.

"Sure. Why not."

He could handle six months of anything. After all, he'd lived in a household that had been pure hell during the time Natália had been undergoing her cancer treatments. He'd never told his sister what he'd found out about their father. And seeing the jerk at her wedding had made a slow boil start up in his gut. It had been part of the reason he'd dragged Sara to the bar that night. To avoid having to interact with the louse that had cheated on his mother and made her cry, who had said terrible things about his sister when she'd been ill.

The folder slid back to Sebastian's side of the desk. "Take this down to Human Resources, then, and tell them that I'm okaying the transfer." The man tapped his pencil on the paper in front of him. "But I'm keeping six months as the maximum, and I'm holding you to these figures. So, keep the costs down as much as you can."

Time for a little last-minute haggling. "I want to be up and running in a week or two."

"A week or two? The ambulance needs to be painted at the very least. I don't want anyone mistaking it for an emergency vehicle, especially if you're taking it into the *favelas*." His lips tightened. "And no narcotics of any kind are to be carried onboard, understood?"

The *favelas* could be dangerous places on a good day,

and if someone thought that they could find drugs inside it would be a recipe for a disaster.

"Understood. I'll make arrangements for the painting." He wasn't going to tell the administrator he already had a body shop lined up. A friend of a friend who was giving him a huge discount on the job.

"If this goes well, it will be great PR for the hospital. So make sure everything runs smoothly. No snafus, got it?"

"I understand." And if there were snafus with Sara? What if she expected to take up where they'd left off at the motel, once she found out she'd be working with him? Although the fact that she'd disappeared before he'd woken up made him think she wouldn't. There'd been no sexy good mornings. No breakfasts in bed. Just an empty motel room.

There would be no snafus. Sebastian would do everything in his power to make sure they were able to work together. As long as she was okay with keeping things purely professional.

And if she wasn't?

Then she might very well make his life difficult. Or at least his job.

So he had to make sure that didn't happen.

No matter how hard it became. At least for the next six months.

Sara was elated. Even though part of her had been dreading this trip for the last week.

Would she run into Sebastian? It had been five and a half weeks since they'd found themselves at that motel together. But they'd both had far too much to drink. He probably didn't even remember that night. Not that she'd waited around to find out.

What did it matter? She had the job! Carrying her small suitcase up the walkway toward the huge modern hospital, she felt like she was coming home. She'd spent almost a year of her life at this place while her dad had undergone treatment—first chemo, and then surgery to replace part of his femur with an internal prosthesis, a surgery she hadn't even known existed before they'd come here. That was when she'd realized how insulated her little world was.

Her dad's care had been first class. His doctors had saved his life. And Natália, the neonatal doctor who had shared her personal story of surviving the same type of cancer, had infused him with the will to try. Sara really believed that. The two had become fast friends over the course of their time there. And if she had to face Natália's brother at her new post, well, she would grit her teeth and bear it. He hadn't tried to contact her since that night, but that was understandable, since she'd been the one to sneak out at the crack of dawn.

Her stomach gave a twinge of nerves, the butterflies she'd felt for the last week developing wings of steel as they flapped around her belly. Her dad was worried about her being this far away from home, but at twenty-six it was well past time she found her own wings and flew away. Even if they were waging war inside her at the moment.

She was pretty sure that in the big city men made love to women and then went on about their lives—wasn't that how things were depicted on television? Thank God she'd never told her father what had happened that night. He would have been firmly against her coming here if he'd known, and it might tarnish his perception of Sebastian. Instead, Sara had simply told him that she'd spent the night with a friend after having one too many drinks.

And she had.

Pushing a buzzer at the entrance, she gave her name to the person who answered. The glass door promptly clicked open and she pushed through it, wiping Sebastian Texeira from her thoughts. At least for now.

The service entrance was well lit, the marble fittings she remembered being in the main corridor were echoed even here. Employees were treated well. You could tell by the care put into the details. They probably had to attract and keep the best talent in the country, so they treated them right. And now she was here. Among the best of the best. A place she'd never thought she'd be. The fact that it was only temporary made her determined to get as much as she could out of the experience. Maybe she would learn something she could introduce to her own hospital back home.

She swung into the door marked "Administration", where she was supposed to meet some of the members of her team. As soon as she entered the room, however, she stopped, her heart stumbling for a beat or two. Sitting in a beige leather chair, one ankle propped on his knee, was the person she had just shoved from her mind. The wings in her belly turned into chainsaws, slashing at her innards and turning them to mush.

"What are you—?" She tried again. "I'm sorry. I'm supposed to meet someone here."

A someone who isn't you.

His long legs uncurled as he stood upright. And he was much taller than she remembered, her neck having to tilt to look into his face, unusual for her. Of course, when you were horizontal, differences in heights didn't— *Stop it!*

"I'm assuming that person is me."

"Excuse me?" Shock streamed through her, washing

away the saws, the wings and anything else that might still be cruising around inside her.

"Not who you were expecting?" His lips thinned, face turning grim. Other than that, not a hint of emotion flickered through those dark eyes. No "Hello, nice to see you again," or "How have you been?"

So that's how he wanted to play this. He was going to pretend he didn't know her. Or maybe he wasn't pretending. Maybe it had meant so little to him that he could just lock it away and hurl the key out into the universe. Something she should be doing as well. Maybe people here in São Paulo were like the hospital: cold and clinical. Wiped clean of anything that didn't belong. Where she came from things were very different. She'd been a willing participant in his little game, so she was going to have to live with the consequences.

She'd wanted this job, had practically gotten down on her knees and begged her little clinic for the opportunity to come once she'd seen the ad go up on the staff bulletin board. So she'd better get over it or she was going to ruin everything.

"You're in charge of the screening program?"

"I am. Partly because of your father."

Her brow furrowed. "I don't understand."

"He made me realize that not everyone recognizes symptoms of illness before they're advanced. I want to help change that by going into the poorer communities and working with people who wouldn't normally come to the hospital."

Her dad had made that happen?

And what about what had happened between her and Sebastian? Should she bring it up?

Why? So he could sit there and wonder if she was hung up on what had happened over the course of a few hours?

No way. If he could act like it hadn't happened, then she damn well could too.

"I'm grateful for this opportunity."

"That's good. Staff at Hospital Santa Coração are already stretched thin. I couldn't ask anyone to take this on pro bono."

"I wasn't aware this was an unpaid position. My understanding was that the *estágio* brought in a stipend. They quoted me a figure." How was she going to support herself if she didn't get paid?

"You're right. It does. You were the only one to apply for the position…" He nodded toward another man in the room that she'd just noticed. That person's eyes were studiously fixed on some document in front of him. "Did you want me to say no?"

He could have. He could have turned her down flat.

She swallowed. He'd said she was the only one who'd applied for the position. So, was she the only one who had raised her hand when he'd been looking for a sleeping partner at the wedding as well? The thought made her feel physically ill.

Doing her best to choke back the sensation, she drew herself up to her full height. "I guess you said yes."

"And so did you." His voice was soft as he said it, his glance studying her in a way that made her tummy ripple.

"Yes, and so did I. I actually thought I'd be working with Dr. Pinheiro, though." So what if they'd slept together? It wasn't like she'd had any expectations of that night other than what had happened.

But a motel? She'd never in her life set foot in one of those establishments and if anyone she knew found out…

They hadn't. She'd crept out early in the morning, while it had still been dark and had asked the desk to call her a taxi, unable to look anyone in the eye. But she'd made it. And the experience had changed her in a way she didn't quite understand.

She'd gotten over her ex-boyfriend once and for all.

"Marcos is the head of oncology. He signs all the request forms for the department. But this project is all mine."

That made her swallow. She would be working with him? Only with him? If she had known that ahead of time, she might not have applied.

The other man looked up finally. "Sorry, I wasn't trying to ignore you. Dr. Texeira has found you a studio apartment in the hospital. Is that okay? Or would you prefer to make other arrangements?"

Like maybe get on the first plane out of here?

"The apartment will be fine, thank you. It doesn't make sense to try to look for something else. I won't have to worry about transportation to or from the hospital this way."

Besides, the rents in many parts of the city were so high she wouldn't be able to afford it on what she'd be making. And although it was comparable to her salary in Rio Grande do Sul, the amount wouldn't go nearly as far here. A thought occurred. Would she have to travel to get to wherever they were going to do the screenings?

"Is there a metro that goes from here to the screening site?"

"No. We have a mobile unit. We'll leave from the hospital together."

"Leave? Together?" Okay, the way she'd separated the words gave them an entirely different meaning from his simple statement.

If he'd heard it, he ignored it, because he didn't hesitate with his answer. "The hospital is converting an old ambulance for us. We'll go to where our patients are, instead of waiting for them to come to us."

The reality of the situation was creating a buzzing noise in her head. She had been told what the job opportunity was and had jumped at the chance. But then again, she hadn't known at the time who she would be working with. And if what he was saying was true, they would be working together much more closely than she'd been expecting.

She'd assumed they would bump into each other periodically. Had even steeled herself for that possibility.

Get a grip, Sara! If it were any other doctor you wouldn't have batted an eyelid.

But it wasn't. It was Sebastian, a man she'd made passionate love with. Surely the hospital didn't approve of workplace romances.

The incident had happened before she knew she was coming here, so that didn't count, right? And since it was never going to happen again, it was a moot point.

And it *was* never going to happen again, even if Sebastian wanted it to. Although right now he looked all business. It didn't matter. He might be able to play loose and easy with relationships, but Sara really wasn't built that way, as was obvious from the way she kept obsessing over the same topic.

"Like you said, that will make it easy, then. I take it you live close by."

He gave a half-smile. "Close enough."

And what was that supposed to mean? She had no idea, but the sooner she got away from him the better. "Well, I guess I have some paperwork to fill out?"

"Yes." He scooped up a file that was on a nearby table. "I have it right here. We can go over it together."

Perfect. That was all she needed, to have to sit next

to him and have him go over things. But she'd better get used to it if she was going to take the job. Because if what he'd told her was true, she was going to be sitting next to him day after day.

Until either the job was done. Or she was.

CHAPTER TWO

THE VEHICLE WAS PERFECT. But not too perfect, given where they'd be working.

Once an ambulance, but now painted a cool silver to reflect the fierce Brazilian heat, it was fully outfitted and ready to go. The hospital's name was not emblazoned on the side, for fear that it would be a target for thieves who were looking for illegal drugs. In fact, there were little nicks in the paintwork and a dent marred one side. A picture of two hands, palms outstretched, was painted in muted colors. Nestled inside them were the words "Mãos Abertos." The name was fitting since the hospital saw it as opening their hands to those in need. Below the hands was a mobile number that would ring through to a special cellphone that Sebastian would carry. Word would get around quickly about what the old ambulance did, and hopefully it would become a symbol of hope.

"What do you think?" he asked Sara, who stood a few yards away.

"It doesn't look like a normal ambulance."

"The hospital didn't want it to. Besides, I'm hoping to take away some of the stigma—the fear of the unknown that comes with emergency vehicles."

Like the time his teenaged sister had been hauled off to the hospital in a flurry of red lights and sirens, while he'd been left at home with his ailing grandmother, wondering if he would ever see her again. Her cancer diagnosis had devastated everyone. But she'd pulled through, thank God. It was one of the reasons Sebastian had gone into oncology.

To help people like his sister. He'd always felt that if she'd been diagnosed earlier maybe she wouldn't have had to have an internal prosthesis in her arm. It was another reason why this mobile unit was his heart's desire.

"So what will we do, exactly?"

"We'll do things never attempted before." Only when her teeth came down on her bottom lip did he realize how that sounded. He was doing his best to keep his cool, but failing miserably. He cleared his throat. "We'll do screenings and teach people what to look for in themselves. We'll check for enlarged thyroids, breast lumps, do pap smears, look for skin cancers. If we find something suspicious, we'll refer them for testing."

"To Santa Coração?"

That was one of the sticking points. Their hospital wasn't part of the public sector, so the administrator would probably balk at them sending dozens of people their way. But Sebastian was already building relationships outside his hospital. Lucas Carvalho, who ran a free clinic inside one of the larger *favelas*, worked with a public hospital as well as Santa Coração. Lucas had agreed to partner with him and use the mobile unit as a springboard to expand his clinic's reach. It was the perfect way to get started. Hopefully as time went on, Lucas could use this as a means to garner donations and grants from outside agencies, since he and his wife traveled with relief groups quite a bit.

"The sister hospital Dr. Carvalho works with is called

Tres Corações. They're willing to take up to fifty patients a month."

"Fifty?" Her eyes widened. "You think we'll refer that many people?"

"Probably not. It depends on how many are willing to be screened. The whole 'ignorance is bliss' attitude is the scourge of most health-care professionals."

"Ignorance is death." Her voice was soft, maybe remembering what Sebastian had once told her father when he'd tried to refuse treatment. Thank God the man had changed his mind—all thanks to his sister's willingness to be vulnerable and share her own story with him. It was exactly what Sebastian was hoping would happen with this unit.

Sara pulled her hair over one of her shoulders, catching the long dark waves together in one hand, the ends sliding over the curve of her breast. It was something he'd seen her do at Natália's wedding as well—he'd been fascinated by the way she'd kept twisting those silky locks. It had taken his mind off his best friend marrying Sebastian's sister, something he still had trouble wrapping his head around.

She twisted the rope of hair tighter. Nervous habit? He wasn't sure, but with her crisp white shirt and dark skirt she was the epitome of a professional nurse, but not quite what he was looking to put forth when they ventured into the neighborhoods. But he wasn't quite sure how to broach the subject without appearing to be dictating what she should and shouldn't wear. It was just that climbing in and out of the back of the ambulance was going to be difficult enough as it was, and it was Sebastian's hope to appear casual and approachable—engender trust where there was normally suspicion.

His gaze traveled down to her feet, where a hole at the

toe of each shoe allowed a glimpse of pink sparkly polish, something that didn't quite fit in with the rest of her attire. She'd had the same sparkly polish on at the wedding. He'd kissed each of those gorgeous toes of hers...

Her hair not being pinned up was another of those little idiosyncrasies. Maybe that's what was with his continued fascination with it. His eyes traveled back up her bare legs.

He definitely didn't want men ogling them as she got in and out of the truck.

Like he'd ogled them that night? And was still ogling them?

No, he was simply trying to decide how to best bring up the subject of their attire.

He'd worn jeans and a dark T-shirt today.

Her fingers twisted the rope of hair yet again and a corresponding knot in his throat formed and then squeezed shut. He swallowed to loosen it. "Do you want to see inside the vehicle?"

Time to get this show on the road and Sara out of his thoughts.

She nodded, moving around to the back with him. When he opened the doors and pulled down the steps he'd had installed for their patients, her brows went up.

"Maybe this isn't the best thing to wear out on runs." She released her hair, the locks tumbling free as her palms ran down the smooth line of her skirt.

Okay, here was his chance. "I think the more casual we are the better, if that's okay. I want people to see us as allies rather than as authority figures. It's why we put a few dents and dings in our vehicle."

She seemed to think about that for a second. "That makes sense. I *guess*."

Her slight hesitation over that last word made him frown. "I'm not sure I follow."

"Will people take us seriously?"

Professionalism was one of the things impressed upon students in medical school, and it was probably the same in the nursing sector. But he'd seen from Lucas's own practice in the *favela* that his friend had fit in and become a fixture in that community. He almost always wore simple, even slightly tattered jeans. Maybe it wasn't his clothing that did it, though. Lucas had been born in that very same *favela*. But Sebastian thought it went deeper than that, and he hoped to be able to build on Lucas's success. Maybe they could be an example to other doctors who would then give their time and talents in other communities. Sebastian had taken a trip into the Amazon several years ago and had worked with a medical missionary who'd traveled to villages providing free health care. It had impacted him deeply.

Almost as deeply as his sister's cancer journey.

And his parents' simmering anger toward each other. And how he'd always felt the need to shield Natália from it.

He guessed he'd done something right, since she'd fallen in love and gotten married. Too bad he'd been the one to see all the ugliness first-hand. It had soured him on relationships and made him suspicious anytime a woman started wandering a little closer than he wanted.

Like Sara?

Totally different situation.

"I would hope so." He climbed the metal steps that led into the back of the truck. "We also have a ramp we can use for people who have trouble climbing stairs. Do you want me to slide it out?"

Her pink lips curved, activating a dimple in her right

cheek. "I grew up on a ranch, remember? I'm actually a tomboy at heart, so wearing jeans will be a welcome relief. I can manage."

Okay, so much for wondering if she was going to be upset about not wearing scrubs or skirts. When her dad was being treated at the hospital, she'd always worn sleek tops and fashionable slacks. And at the wedding she'd looked like every man's dream.

And she'd been his for a single heady night.

As for tomboy, he wasn't sure he'd ever seen her in jeans. But now that he thought about it, the description might not be so off the mark. It was there in the loose-limbed way she walked. In the slight twang to her words. Maybe she'd felt she had to dress to match the hospital's fancy decor.

Sara put her first foot on the bottom step, the narrow skirt tightening and exposing a pale knee. Her skin was fairer than that of most of the women he knew, maybe because Rio Grande do Sul had a large contingent of people with German ancestry. Her hair was dark, though.

"Okay, so a handrail might be useful for women who come for screening wearing skirts or dresses." She paused.

He got the hint, reaching a hand toward her. Her fingers wrapped around his, and she made short work of the other three steps, coming to stand within inches of him. He released his grip in a hurry. "Point taken. I'll have one installed."

Anything to avoid having to touch her each time she went up or down those steps. Something about the way she stood in front of him...

An image flashed through his head of a woman straddling his hips, laughing down into his face at something he'd said, his words slurring slightly due to the amount of alcohol he'd consumed. The sensation of being squeezed. Soft hands with a firm grip, just like hers had been a second ago.

His brain went on hyperdrive.

What was wrong with *him*?

Then, almost without volition, the words came out. "Why did you leave that night?"

Something in her eyes flashed, and she suddenly grabbed for the metal edge of the ambulance's door opening.

Afraid she might fall out of the back—or turn and flee—he wrapped an arm around her waist and turned them both ninety degrees, the narrow aisle providing precious little room between their bodies. But it also meant she couldn't run away.

"I have no idea what you're talking about." Her face had gone white.

Maybe she didn't even remember the events of that night. Except something about the way those words had shot out of her mouth said she did. Along with her horrified expression. A stab of regret speared through his gut. He remembered most of it. But her leaving without saying goodbye bothered him somehow. Had he done something awful?

His jaws clamped together for several tense seconds while he tried to figure out what to say to make this right. He came up empty.

"I think you know exactly what I'm talking about. Are you okay?" Realizing his arm was still around her, he let it drop to his side.

Right on cue, her chin went up as if daring him to say anything further. "I'm fine. My father doesn't know, though, so I'd prefer you not to discuss it with him or anyone else. We both agreed it was one night. No strings. No regrets."

So why was he feeling a whole lot of that right now?

That warning about not discussing it was completely unnecessary, though. He wasn't about to go trumpeting it to her father, or to anyone else for that matter. "I would rather keep it that way as well."

His head was reeling, still trying to blot out the more explicit images from that night. As drunk as he'd been, he should remember a whole lot less than he did.

"You still didn't answer the question. Why did you leave?"

"Um—because I wanted to. I would just as soon for-get it ever happened."

Maybe he really had done something horrible at the end? Passed out on her? Thrown up? Been unable to perform?

No. He could remember each of those performances in stunning detail. Three encores, to be exact. And noth-ing horrific in any of those memories.

And could there be a more self-centered list of things to be worried about? He didn't think so—except for one glaring issue.

"We used…" he forced himself to spit the word out, changing the term at the last second "…protection. So we're covered, right?"

"You don't remember?"

He wasn't sure what she was asking. *Merda!* He did not want to be having this conversation.

"Yes, but we'd both had a lot to drink. I wanted to make sure." And if that wasn't the lamest excuse ever.

"We're good. There's nothing to be worried about."

But he was, for some unfathomable reason. He tried to find the cause—decided to settle for the truth. "I wasn't that thrilled that my sister was getting married." He shrugged. "I never saw it coming, actually, and when she fell in love with my best friend, I was... Well, I acted like a jerk."

"Do tell." The dryness of the words made him laugh.

"Shocking, I know."

Her dimple appeared again. "Not so much."

He took a deep breath, the urge to reach up and touch her sliding through him. He forced it back. "I'm sorry I dragged you along on my little joy ride of misery. Believe it or not, I don't normally drink. Or seduce wedding guests."

Mainly because his father had done a lot of that. His parents had battled relentlessly all during his sister's illness. He'd finally realized they didn't love each other—his dad's dalliances proved that beyond a shadow of a doubt. They had simply been staying together for their children—more specifically for Natália, because of her illness. It was one reason Sebastian had basically sworn off marriage and children. What if it didn't last? Would he follow his parents' example and stay in a miserable marriage because of any offspring he might have? They'd already been expecting him when they'd got married. He knew that for a fact. Sebastian, like most children, was attuned to whether his parents loved and respected each other—or when they didn't.

"You didn't have to seduce me. I wanted to go. Even though, I've never..." her smile faded "...spent the night at a motel with someone I barely know."

A few more curse words tumbled around in his head. Had she been a virgin?

Before he could ask, she shook her head. "No, not because of that. I just don't normally go to motels. Especially not with a stranger."

Neither did he.

They knew each other in a superficial way because of her father, but for all intents and purposes she was right.

"Hell, Sara, I'm sorry. I have no idea what—"

She stopped his words with a raised hand. "Don't. It's over and done with. Let's just do our jobs and keep the past where it belongs—in the past."

Much easier said than done. And if the flashes of memory kept replaying in his head every time they worked together?

Well, he would just do what she'd suggested and put it behind him. Except Sara was standing in front of him looking too beautiful for words. A shaft of sunlight ventured in through the open door and touched the hair over her left shoulder, infusing the strands with gold. The sight tugged at something inside him.

"You're right. I'll try not to mention it again. Or even think about it." Those last words came out rough-edged, and he knew they were a lie. He'd already been thinking about it. And his body was torturing him with whether or not they might be able to do any of those things again.

No. They couldn't.

"Neither will I." Her voice was soft. Almost a whisper. As if she sensed the turmoil that was chewing up his gut and was answering it with some of her own.

Not good. Because his gaze slid to her lips. Came back up to her eyes, where he saw it. The slightest shimmer of heat beneath the cool brown irises.

"We'll put it behind us."

"Absolutely."

"Starting right now."

"Yes." The tip of her tongue peeked out, moistening her lips before darting back in. He wanted to follow it. Find it.

No, this was not good. Only it had been. Far too good.

He gave a pained groan.

"Sara?" His palms came up and cupped her cheeks, relishing the cool softness of her skin against his.

"Yes."

There was no question mark after that single word. No "Yes? What do you want?" It was more like she'd breathed, "Kiss me. It's what we both want."

It had been what they'd both wanted on that fateful night.

He wanted it to happen again, his body already responding to the stimuli of having her this close. And it was too much.

Tilting her face, he met her halfway, his mouth covering hers in a way that muttered, *Home. Finally.*

Even though it wasn't. It was merely a stopping place.

But, damn, the burst of steam that zipped through his veins erased that notion in a split second. He suddenly didn't care about stopping places or anything else. Instead, he shifted so that the angle was perfect.

And it was. Her lips were warm and giving and the tongue that had played peek-a-boo with his senses a second ago was back, coaxing him to sneak away with her, luring him just like those sirens of old. Without hesitation he ducked inside, finding heat and wetness that shoved his body further down a forbidden road, a growing pressure behind his zipper impossible to ignore.

Sara's hands went behind his back and slid upward until they curved around his shoulders, her body coming into full contact with his.

Maybe she felt the same sudden urgency that he did.

It was only when one of his hands left her face to pull the door next to him shut, only to have it bounce off

something with a loud *clang,* that he realized how far
gone he was. How far gone they both were.

Their lips came apart at exactly the same time, Sara
being the first to come to her senses, uncurling her arms
and pushing at his chest.

He released her and tried to take a step back, but his
butt hit the metal counter behind him, stopping him from
retreating any further.

Her mouth was pink and moist, lips still parted as she
drew in several breaths.

He glanced to the side to see what had happened with
the door and realized the metal steps had stopped it from
closing.

Graças a Deus. Because otherwise…

What exactly would he have done? Tossed her onto
that counter and made love to her? In the hospital parking garage?

What the hell had he been thinking?

He hadn't been. That was the problem. Just like the
night of the wedding. He'd been operating off pure lust.

Gripping that very same metal counter, he tried to get
his bearings. Saying he was sorry was going to be met
with angry words. But what else could he do?

"I take it that wasn't what you meant by 'putting this
behind us'." She tossed her hair back over her shoulder.

"Not exactly. No."

"So what do we do? I worked hard to get this *estágio,*
and I'm not going to let a little thing like this make me
run home with my tail tucked between my legs."

A little thing like this? This was pretty damn huge in
his book. He never mixed work with personal stuff. Ever.
It was just the shock of being alone with her again. But
it stopped right here.

"I would never ask you to go home. You're here, and so am I. This project can't go forward without both of us, so we are going to have to figure this thing out. Fast."

"And how do you propose we do that?"

"By making sure we are alone as little as humanly possible."

She blinked. "Isn't that a little unrealistic? We'll be driving around together in this thing—alone—in order to do our jobs."

Maybe, but right now it was the only way. Because his head was still wrapped around the taste of her, the scent of her hair, the sounds of her breathing as they'd been fused together. "If you can think of a better option, I'm all ears."

And mouth. And raging hormones.

She bit her lip. "I can't."

Neither could he. He was appalled that his body had responded with an immediacy that had yanked him from that fully-in-control-but-fake-as-hell persona he liked to cloak himself in. It had exposed the true Sebastian Texeira. And he didn't like it. At all.

"We can still do this. We have to do this. Otherwise I might as well turn this mobile center back over to the hospital and forget I ever asked for the funds to try."

"Which means there would be no reason for me to stay in São Paulo." Her eyes sought his. "The hospital wouldn't keep me on?"

"I could talk to them and ask—"

"No. I want to do this. I need to do this."

"Why?" He wasn't quite sure what had driven her to come here. She'd probably made more money in Rio Grande do Sul.

"When my dad was sick, I realized how isolated my

little hospital was. Doing things the same way as they'd been doing them for decades. I want to make a difference."

"I'm sure you already have."

She shrugged. "Maybe, but I saw the effect you, Natália and Adam had on my father. I want to be a part of something like that. To take back new ideas and ways of doing things." She motioned around the inside of the truck. "This is exactly what I've been looking for. And I'm not going to let an embarrassing lapse in judgment stand in the way of that. Neither one of us should, if you're as serious as I think you are about doing this."

"I am."

"Then let's focus on that, okay?"

She was right. He knew she was.

The only thing left was to get his body to agree to forget this "lapse in judgment", as she'd put it, had ever happened.

Only he knew that was going to be almost impossible.

So he was just going to have to pull that cloak tighter and pretend. And hope to God that Sara never saw the truth.

CHAPTER THREE

SIX WEEKS.

That time frame rattled around in her head over and over as she sat in the cab of the truck beside Sebastian.

Stress. A change of jobs.

Working with a man she'd slept with.

Slept. With.

Those two words linked arms with the other two words and began to dance a little jig in her stomach. Right beside the butterflies that had never left.

Six weeks.

She couldn't be. They'd used protection. All three times.

Oh, God.

"Have you ever visited a *favela*?"

The question slid past her before turning in a smooth circle and coming back at her. "I'm sorry?"

He glanced at her with a frown. "I asked if you'd ever been to a *favela*."

"Yes." She blinked back the growing fear. "I think all cities have some kind of slum. There was one a few miles from our house. It was fairly safe—run by a group of women who decided to fight back against the image that all *favelas* are dangerous, drug-infested places. They had to give the okay for anyone new to move in."

"This one is not like that. It has had—and still does

have—a drug presence. You'll need to be on the lookout for any unusual activity."

She was. Only that unusual activity wasn't happening outside the windows of the mobile unit. It was happening deep inside her body. And there was a sense of panic that said the unthinkable could very well be reality.

But it couldn't. It was—while not impossible, it was highly unlikely.

Except hadn't she read recently about a spate of condom tamperings across the country? A fad where kids dared each other to go into stores unnoticed and stab pinholes in packages? It had caused an uptick in unwanted pregnancies. And STDs.

Deus. STDs. An even stronger spurt of alarm went through her.

Surely she was safe. The condoms had been provided by the motel. There were quality control checks. There had to be.

At a *motel*?

Those establishments were gorgeous on the outside with their high walls, beautiful signs and manicured landscapes. But the elegant facade hid what really went on behind the entry gate. Sex. Lots of it. Mostly between people who weren't married—or who were, but not to each other.

It's okay. You're overreacting. It's an easy thing to check.

Except she had to endure the entire work day before she could get to a *farmácia* to buy a pregnancy test.

She realized he was waiting for a response. "Don't worry. I'll make sure I'm aware of my surroundings. Aren't we going to your friend's clinic?"

"No. We may at some point, but Lucas has already set up a couple of appointments at people's homes. One of them is an elderly lady who rarely leaves her house and can't make it to the clinic. The other appointment concerns a child."

"A child? We're doing screening on a kid?"

"Yes. He's evidently had a lump in his neck that's been there for a while."

"An infection?"

He glanced her way again. "We can hope so."

A reminder that there were more important things out there than her churning stomach right now. She would do well to remember that.

They reached the entrance to the *favela,* and Sara smoothed her palms over her dark-washed jeans. It seemed so strange to not have on her normal scrubs or business attire. It felt like she was simply going out to visit friends. Only none of her friends lived in a neighborhood like this one.

Ramshackle homes made of plywood boards hastily nailed together to form a box were scattered around. Some of the "nicer" places were constructed of bare clay bricks. None of them had seen the business end of a spackle float or a paintbrush. Roofs were either blue tarps held down by more of the same crude bricks or clay tiles. The roads were the same red clay. It could have been a neighborhood on the red planet, it was that foreign-looking to Sara.

He thrust a piece of paper at her. "Does your cellphone have GPS?"

"Yes." She glanced at the address and then reached into her purse for her phone. Then she made short work of punching the address in and waiting as the service pinpointed their location and looked for the destination.

"In thirty meters, turn right onto Viscaya, then turn left."

The neutral computer voice did more to calm her nerves than anything else that had happened today. The voice wasn't worried. About anything.

She shouldn't worry either. It was just an upset in her hormonal system. That was all. She relaxed back against the seat. She was here to do a job. A role she was comfortable with. Or at least should be.

Sebastian concentrated on navigating through the narrow streets, their truck seeming huge compared to the bicycles and motorcycles parked at odd angles. For the first time she was glad they'd played down the appearance of their vehicle.

"Have you been to many of these?" she asked.

He didn't seem like the type of person who popped in and out of a slum on a daily basis.

What about a motel? How many of those had he been to?

This is ridiculous. Stop it already!

"I've been to a few. And I've covered for Lucas at his clinic several times when he was on vacation."

"And you've never had a problem?"

"No. Despite the drug problem, *favelas* have a kind of internal code on who is and isn't welcome." His hands tightened on the wheel. "I guarantee if we came in here with a police car, the reception would be very different."

She swallowed. He must have sensed the trickle of fear that went through her because he continued. "Lucas has made sure people know who we are. They've already had eyes on us, but no one has given us any grief."

"They have? I haven't noticed anyone."

"And you probably won't." Up went his brows. "Are you sorry you came to São Paulo yet?"

Was she? Actually, she wasn't. "No, I'm just trying to be aware of my surroundings, like you asked me to be."

"Great."

"So whose house are we going to first?"

Neither of them had mentioned what had happened a week ago in the back of this very vehicle. As the hospital finished outfitting the mobile unit, Sara had unpacked and tried to get settled, dreading having to actually go out with him and receive patients. But it was either that or admit defeat, and she wasn't one who gave up. Not easily anyway.

Her phone gave another set of instructions, listing the next street as their destination.

"We're going to the shut-in's place first. She has a lump in her breast."

That surprised her. Not the part about the lump but about them tackling that kind of screening. "I don't remember seeing a mammogram machine back there."

Not that she remembered seeing much of anything outside Sebastian's face and the feel of his mouth on hers.

And that was a very inappropriate thought.

"We don't, but we have portable ultrasound equipment."

"You can tell from that?"

He gazed at the row of houses, slowing down slightly. Some of them had numbers painted on them in crude lettering, but some of them didn't. "I can't tell if something is malignant, not with any certainty. But I can tell by the way it registers on the ultrasound what kind of lump it is. We want to see a fluid-filled pocket rather than a solid mass. It won't be definitive, but without being able to force anyone to go to the hospital for check-ups, it's the best we can do. It has a pretty good track record."

"How old is the patient?"

He nudged a couple of files toward her. "She should be in here somewhere."

"Name?"

"Talita Moises. I think she's seventy-eight."

Flipping through the names on the tabs, she found the patient without much difficulty. But when she opened it, there were no neat, computer-generated forms inside. Instead there was a wrinkled piece of paper that looked like it had been torn from a notebook. The patient's name, age and complaint were scribbled on it. "We're not going to keep actual records?"

"Yes. But we'll only do up paperwork for patients we actually treat. Some of them might refuse to be seen. I have a micro recorder that I'll use to take notes. I'll have it transcribed later."

Was that going to be part of her duties? A lot of times nurses acted almost like secretaries, entering diagnoses and listing findings.

"Um, okay."

"You won't have to do that, if that's what you're worried about."

"No, not worried at all. I'll do whatever you need me to do."

Including carrying his child?

The thought entered her head unbidden and her face became a scorching hot mess.

He glanced sideways at her. "Are you okay?"

"Hot flash."

One side of his mouth tilted. "A little young for that, aren't you?"

When this man was around, she wouldn't put anything past her body. She'd had sex with him, for heaven's sake. Something she was still having trouble accepting. She'd only slept with her boyfriend after months of dating.

"We live in Brazil. I think everyone is subject to them from time to time."

His grin tipped higher. "Indeed."

With that, he shut the engine off. "I'll get the equipment."

"I'll go up and ring the bell."

"No. You won't. We don't go up to any doors unaccompanied. We do everything together."

Yes. They had.

She gulped. *Céus.* She'd better stop with all the double meanings. "Is that really necessary?"

"It is. You never know who is going to open that door."

"And you would do what, if some crazed drug dealer appeared brandishing a gun?"

"I would try to talk my way out of the situation."

"And you don't think I could do that?"

His fingers covered hers for a second, the warm grip slightly tighter than necessary. "Yes, I think you could do that. It's just safer—for both of us—if we stick together."

Sara was all for staying safe. Which was why she'd handed him a second condom when the time had come. And a third.

Why? Why are you insisting on thinking about this?

"Okay. I'll help you carry the equipment, then."

As they both climbed into the back of the truck, Sara took the opportunity to look around this time. A metal counter along one wall held an assortment of containers that were wedged into holders so they wouldn't spill all over the place. The standard tongue depressors, rubbing alcohol and cotton balls were all neatly tucked away. And it looked like beneath the counter there was a— She fingered the metal edge of whatever it was.

"Yes, it's an exam table, in case we need to look at someone or draw blood."

"There's barely room in here for us as it is. How are we going to work around something like that?"

"It's gurney sized. It'll be a tight fit, but we'll manage."

Damn. Her brain wasn't even going to try to tackle that one. "Okay, and the ultrasound machine?"

"Right inside that blue box."

A tackle box thing was clamped to the wall, a wooden peg supporting the machine's handle. "Wow."

Sara was seriously impressed. "How many things can we screen for?"

"A lot. Especially if we can draw blood from our patients. We have a mini-fridge just beneath the legs of the pull-out exam table where we can store samples until we get them back to the lab for testing."

A spurt of pride went through her, erasing all the little quivers of fear she'd had ever since she'd climbed back into the truck with him. They could actually make a difference here. Just like she'd hoped. All she had to do was keep her mind focused on that fact, and off a certain handsome doctor. Not an easy task. But she could do it. She knew she could.

"What do you want me to take?"

"I'll take the sonogram machine and laptop so we can view the images, if you'll reach under that cabinet and grab the red soft sided bag. It has the lubricant for the wand and some other items we might need."

She wrapped her fingers around the handle on the only cabinet in the place when he stopped her. "Here's the key."

She took it, noticing the lock. "I thought you said we weren't carrying anything with narcotics in it."

"We're not carrying much of anything, but there are syringes in there for blood collection. Sometimes it's better to keep temptation behind lock and key."

Yes. It was. Too bad she hadn't thought of that the

night of Natália's wedding. She could have locked her heart up and thrown away the key.

Although her heart hadn't been involved in that little encounter, right?

No, just parts of her body. She hoped nothing more than those pleasure centers had been activated that night.

Carrying that thought with her as they hauled their equipment up the dirt walkway, she asked, "Is she not mobile enough to come out to the truck?"

"I don't know. But I didn't want to take any chances. The only thing Lucas left me was that piece of paper, which is sometimes all the information he has."

He raised his hands and clapped three times. Doorbells were reserved for people in wealthier areas. In poor neighborhoods—actually, even at Sara's dad's house because of the migrant workers they often hired—they still gave that staccato series of claps to announce their presence. Even though they'd had a doorbell ever since she could remember.

The door opened and a tall gangly boy with dark eyes appeared. *"Quem é?"*

"We're here to see Dona Talita Moises. Lucas Carvalho sent us. Is she home?"

"Sim. Minha avó está por aqui." He motioned them inside, instead of calling his grandmother to the entrance, which surprised Sara. Maybe they weren't as wary of strangers here as Sebastian claimed.

They went into a living room, and then she immediately saw why they'd been summoned inside. A frail woman with a shock of gray hair sat on a stained floral chair. She wore a blue checked house dress, and unless one of her legs was tucked beneath her... It wasn't. It was missing. She swallowed, remembering her father's cancer and what could have happened if they hadn't been able to get him in for an appointment at Hospital Santa Coração. He could have been sitting on a chair very much like this one.

No, he wouldn't have been. Because he would have refused treatment. A die-hard cowboy whose entire existence was measured in how many kilometers he'd ridden that day, he'd somehow had the notion that his life wouldn't mean anything if he couldn't ride his horse or work his cattle. But people had survived much worse than that and found ways to make their lives count.

Sebastian was already introducing himself and Sara to the woman. Talita Moises' shrewd eyes took in their appearance, making her very glad that she was wearing clothing that didn't scream money. Not that she had that many expensive pieces, but even the little she did have were far beyond the means of this household.

She reached out to shake the woman's hand, finding Ms. Moises' grip tight and unyielding. So much so that she couldn't simply pull away from her. Instead the woman studied her. "You are his wife?"

Her brain stumbled over the question for a second before realizing that—

"No!" The denial bounced around the room with such force that Sebastian's head cranked around to look at her. She softened her voice. "I'm a nurse. I just started at the—at this job." She wasn't sure if Sebastian wanted the name of the hospital announced to everyone, since it could be seen as a symbol of the chasm between this community and neighborhoods that were able to afford the insurance necessary to go to a place like Santa Coração.

The woman grunted a sound that could have been an affirmation or a protest, she wasn't sure which. But at least she'd released her death grip on Sara's hand. For some reason the woman made her nervous, and it had nothing to do with where she lived.

"Lucas Carvalho spoke with you about us coming?"

She nodded and then motioned her grandson to make himself scarce. He left the room, the snapping of his flip flops across the tile floor the only sound for a minute or two. And then it too was gone.

Sebastian sat across from her. "How can we help?"

"Well, I found a…I found a bump on…" Her hand made a circling motion over her left breast. "I've already lost my leg. I'm not sure I want to lose anything else."

"No one said anything about losing something. We're just here to check on it, if you're okay with that."

The woman's head gave a snapping nod. "I have diabetes. Maybe that's what's causing it."

Sara didn't want to tell her that it was doubtful that blood sugar issues had caused a lump in her breast. But the loss of her leg? Probably. It could also complicate surgery, if it came to that.

"Have you been undergoing any treatment?"

Talita's laugh came across like the sound of crumpling tinfoil. "Gave myself a shot in the leg every night. Except it didn't do much good. One of them is still gone."

Sara was out of her depth here. She had no idea what to say or do. Was the woman saying she no longer even tried to control her blood sugar levels?

Maybe this hadn't been the right move after all. What exactly did she think she was doing by coming to São Paulo?

It's your first case. Don't judge everything by just one patient.

That last phrase had been pounded into her head during nursing school. But it was hard not to. In a hospital setting she could slip into a familiar role that everyone expected her to play—and she played it well. So well that stepping outside that box made it hard to breathe—to think, let alone come up with some kind of comforting words.

Because if the woman did have cancer, could it even be treated?

Unlike her own chaotic thoughts, Sebastian went through a calm series of questions that had to be second nature to him. Or maybe he was just inured to the heartbreak of a cancer diagnosis. Somehow, she didn't think so, though.

Sebastian cared.

For his patients, at least. The women he slept with? Well, that was another matter. Big city men were no different than men where she came from except people tended to make a bigger deal out of things, since the pool of available dates was much smaller.

Maybe that was why her ex had been able to slip away without a twinge of conscience. He was from one of the larger cities up north, but had come down to help her father with several cattle auctions. Once those were done? *Poof!* Just like a genie retreating back to its bottle.

Her parents' marriage, on the other hand, had been rock solid. No hint that they'd had to settle for whomever had been available.

That was because they'd fallen in love.

Something Sara had once hoped to do. But right now she was resigned to being alone.

Her hand went to her stomach when it gave an odd twist. Oh, God, if she was pregnant, she wasn't going to be alone for long.

Really? She would be more alone than ever, because there would be no one to share her burden.

Her dad would. But Sebastian?

"Sara, could you help Ms. Moises strip out of her blouse and bra, please?"

And just like that, she was back on duty. Maybe Sebastian had sensed her unease and misread the cause of it. Whatever it was, she was just glad to have something to do that didn't involve thinking about everything that could go wrong but probably wouldn't.

Besides, this woman's life was far more important than anything she was currently worried about. "Of course."

"I'll get set up over in the corner and then bring the machine over on the portable gurney. Let me know when you're ready for me."

Thank goodness the grandmother had shooed her grandson to his own room and told him to stay there for an hour or until she called. "Let's get this over with," she grunted.

It was as if the woman was resigned to her fate. Kind of like Sara had been moments earlier. But who would take care of Talita's grandson if she gave up? "What's your grandson's name? He seems like a nice boy."

"His name is Jorge. And yes. He is." The woman sighed as she unbuttoned her blouse and dropped it from her shoulders. "His mother—my daughter—died of a drug overdose five years ago. So I've been doing my best to raise him. But really he helps me more than I help him."

"I very much doubt that. Does he go to school?"

"He's in his fifth year. His grades are some of the highest in his class." The pride in her voice was evident.

"Thanks to your help, I'll bet."

Ms. Moises reached around to unhook her bra, but hesitated, her hand going to her left breast. "There's a hole..."

A hole. Oh, Lord.

That was bad. If it *was* cancer and had broken through the skin...

"Wait right here for a minute, okay? I want to see if the doctor needs anything."

What Sara really wanted was to warn him that he probably was not going to need the ultrasound machine after all. She went over to where he was arranging the equipment.

Careful to keep her voice low, she said, "Whatever it is has turned into an open wound."

A soft curse met her ears. Before he could say anything, she hurried to finish. "I—I want to let her maintain as much of her dignity as possible."

"Agreed. Good job, by the way." His gaze softened. "Okay. I'm going to need you to go back to the truck and get me some gauze. We may need to transport her."

"She's raising her grandson. I doubt she'll let us take her anywhere."

He gave her a sharp look. "You suggest we just leave her here?"

Sara wasn't sure what she was suggesting. "No, I'm just not sure—"

"Go get the gauze, and I'll talk to her."

Her sense of nausea increased tenfold. She was already screwing this up and she hadn't even been on the job for a week yet. Then his hand landed on her shoulder. "You're doing fine."

She sucked down a calming breath and glanced into his face. "Thank you."

By the time she got back with gauze, saline solution and some antibiotic ointment that they had on the truck, Sebastian was on a stool in front of their patient. On his face was a look of fierce concentration. The woman's bra had not come off yet. Maybe Sebastian had been waiting for her return, since a male doctor normally had someone there with him when examining a patient.

She threw a small protective cover on the table next to the woman's chair and then set the items she'd brought on top of it.

"Okay, are you ready?"

Talita nodded, the thin set of her lips showing just how tense she was.

Sara snapped on gloves and then helped the woman peel the bra away. "I'm going to go slowly, if that's okay. I don't want to damage your skin."

"I think the damage has already been done." Talita looked up at them. "I'm not worried about me. I'm worried about Jorge. If I die…"

Her voice trailed away, but it was obvious what she had been going to say. It was exactly the same thing that Sara had thought.

"Let's not worry about that now," said Sebastian. He nodded at Sara to go ahead.

Carefully she eased the layers away to reveal a hole the size of a small coin on the outer edge of her breast, right where her arm would lie. It could be due to infection. Or, worse, cancer.

Sebastian shoved his hands into his own set of gloves and examined the wound, palpating the tissue around the area. He didn't say anything, but Sara could almost see the wheels turning as he tried to sort through possibilities. "I want to go ahead and set up the ultrasound, but I want to disinfect the skin and cover the wand so there's no transfer. We'll also change into new gloves."

Transfer. So he did suspect there was at least some kind of bacteria inside the tissue, or else he was going with an abundance of caution. She could only imagine what would happen if their mobile center became con-

taminated by MRSA or one of the other multi-drug-re-
sistant bacteria. While he prepped the patient for the
procedure, he asked Sara to set up the machine. Thank
goodness she had done a pretty long stint inside the maternity ward at her hospital, so she at least knew the ba-
sics of getting it ready. She calibrated it to the tissue depth
that Sebastian shot off to her, and laid the components
on the sterile pad, ready for Sebastian to use.

Fifteen minutes later, he ran the transponder over the
woman's breast while Sara did her best to engage her in
conversation, hoping to keep her mind off what was happening. She learned that Talita had become a widow at
the young age of nineteen and had been left to raise her
and her husband's only child—a daughter named Marisa.
She had worked three jobs to try to support them but,
having been raised in a *favela* herself, she'd found it almost impossible to rise up out of the narrow streets. And
now she was raising her grandson all by herself.

Sebastian interrupted them. "Did you have any kind
of procedure done on your breasts?"

"Procedure? Like what?"

"Breast augmentation, maybe?"

"Aug—what?"

"Did you have them enlarged?"

The woman's eyes grew wide. "No, of course not. I
could never afford such a thing."

"I could have sworn…" His brows were pulled together. "Did you ever have anything injected into them?"

"No, I haven't—" Suddenly her teeth bit her lip for
several seconds. "Many years ago when I was a young
woman there was this party some girls talked about. I
was very self-conscious about how slowly I was developing…I was very small back then, even after having
my daughter.

"A priestess—a *Mãe-de-Santo*—said there was a safe and easy way to make them grow. She could do it right there inside her house. I went along with it because some of my friends were going to have it done. She gave us each a large shot. One on each side. I don't know what it was—other than it really hurt. But she was right. It instantly made us bigger."

Sebastian shot a quick glance her way. "Silicone."

She'd injected silicone into her breasts? And someone had told her it was safe?

Sara knew that what appeared safe and easy wasn't always. In fact, it was something she was having to learn all over again.

"You think the silicone had something to do with this?"

"I've seen a couple of cases of sclerosing lipogranuloma that mimicked cancer."

"Sclerosing lipogranuloma? I've never even heard of it."

Talita tilted her head. "I don't have cancer, then?"

"I don't think so. I want to get you into a clinic where we can check for sure, but silicone—or another substance—injected directly into tissues can sometimes cause a bad reaction. Kind of like globs of fat that turn into lumps. They can sometimes get infected."

"But that was so long ago."

"It sometimes takes decades before the reaction is enough to be noticeable. And it doesn't happen to everyone."

Sebastian put down the transponder wand and set about bandaging her up. "I want to check to be sure. It might still require surgery."

"No. No surgery."

Sara touched her arm. "Jorge needs you. You said it yourself."

"Would they lop them off? Like my leg?"

Sebastian nodded to Sara to help her get dressed. "It depends on how widespread the problem is. You could eventually develop more of these. Or none. But if you get them taken care of, you can live a long life. Finish raising your grandson. I think you both deserve that."

The woman rubbed a palm across her eyes with a forced casualness that belied far deeper emotions. It was as if Sebastian had just given her back her life. And maybe he had. At the very least, he'd replaced fear with hope. Just like he'd done with Sara's dad.

And glancing over at this enigmatic surgeon, she couldn't help but wonder if he had done the same for her, only in reverse. What had started out as hope for a new job, a new beginning, and a chance to help people like her dad was slowly being swallowed up by fear. The very real fear that Sebastian Texeira might have unintentionally changed her life forever—and the fear of his reaction if it ended up being true.

CHAPTER FOUR

HIS NEW NURSE was late to work. Already.

Not a good omen for their future work relationship. He and Sara were supposed to spend one day a week out in their mobile clinic. The rest of the time she did work in the oncology ward at the hospital, which was where she was supposed to be today.

Had she decided it was all too much for her and thrown in the towel? Leaving without so much as a goodbye? She'd done that very thing after they'd spent the night together. It hadn't seemed like her back then, it didn't seem like her today. Then again, people had surprised him before.

Like his dad with his philandering. Or Sebastian's playboy best friend settling down and marrying Natália.

Could she have left?

Her first day spent in the mobile unit had been a kind of trial by fire with Talita Moises and the little boy with a swelling in his neck. The swelling had turned out to be an inflamed lymph node. All in all, he thought everything had gone well. To an oncologist, any day that brought news of survival was a good day. They had connected Ms. Moises with the doctors at Lucas Carvalho's hospital and things were underway for scheduling surgery. One that might not mean the removal of her breasts. Even if it did, she would live.

Definitely a good day.

So where was Sara?

A niggle of worry settled in his gut.

Just as he was getting ready to check to make sure he'd read the schedule correctly, she came hurrying around the corner, her fingers fiddling with her hair, which was in a high ponytail. Relief warred with irritation. She was due at work and she was worried about how her hair looked?

She stopped directly in front of him, her eyes not quite meeting his. "Sorry. I know I'm late."

"You are." He wasn't about to admit he'd been envisioning her scrambling to catch the first flight home. "Most people around here will tell you that I'm a stickler for punctuality."

"Something came up."

"An emergency?"

"Yes. No." Her face was flushed, beads of perspiration lining her upper lip.

His relief morphed into genuine concern. "Is everything okay?"

She still wasn't looking at him. "No, it's not."

"Your father?"

Although Antônio Moreira's cancer treatments were over, something could always go wrong. Or there were accidents. And since he was a cowboy, there were any number of things that could happen.

"He's fine." Brown eyes met his with a jolt before closing. Reopening. "Is there someplace we can go to talk?"

"Are you quitting the hospital?" Maybe he'd been right after all.

"I'm not sure. I just really need… I really would like to talk to you."

"Let's go to my office." If she had a problem with him, he should be sending her down to Human Resources or to the hospital administrator, but he wanted to hash this out face to face. Why would she quit? She'd only just gotten there, and even though they'd almost kissed in the back of the mobile unit, she'd given no indication that it made a difference. So what was going on?

He led her down a short hallway, opened the door to his office and motioned her inside. Rather than taking a seat behind the desk, he stood in front of it, resting his right hip against the solid surface, suddenly sure he needed the extra support. "So what's this all about? Does it have something to do with your reasons for being late?"

"Yes. I was... I haven't been feeling..." She stopped, her hands squeezed together in front of her. "I'm—I'm pregnant."

There was silence in the room for about five seconds before a slurry of something ugly oozed through his head. She was pregnant? He could have sworn she wasn't the kind of girl who slept around, but maybe he was wrong. Or, worse, maybe sex with him had been an effort to make a boyfriend jealous.

"Does the father know?"

She blinked a couple of times before her gaze hardened, lips thinning dangerously. "He does now."

He tried to process that and failed. "And he wants you to quit, is that it?"

"I don't know. I haven't asked him yet." Her chin went up. "Do you want me to quit?"

"I'm not the one you should be asking. But I'll certainly understand if..." His words faded away as a little thought in the back of his head appeared out of nowhere. He stared at her, willing her to be a mirage—for this whole meeting to be some kind of sick joke.

"You'll certainly understand if what?" Her face was stiff, quiet—almost as if a sculptor had carved a gorgeous image and then encased it in a block of ice.

The hatching thought grew into an adult-sized idea within a few more seconds. "What exactly are you trying to say, Sara?"

"Haven't you figured it out yet?" Her hands were still clasped, knuckles white. "I am pregnant. And you—you are the father."

Father. *Father?*

Uh, no. That isn't right. Can't be right.

Nausea roiled through his gut, spinning in all directions until he was no longer sure what was what. He gripped the desk beside him. "I'm the what?"

"You heard me. I'm pregnant." She licked her lips. "And there hasn't been anyone else. Not since that night."

"Are you sure?"

Her brows went up. "Am I sure there hasn't been anyone else? Pretty damned sure. I think that's something I would remember."

"What's that supposed to mean?" He didn't know why he even asked that question, so he squelched anything that might have followed. But they'd used—

"But that's not possible. I sure as hell found the evidence of protection in that room."

She opened her purse and pulled out a pink stick. "I have some evidence too."

A pregnancy test. On the little readout was a pink plus sign as plain as day. "It could be a false positive."

"Would you like me to show you the other five tests? I can go get them from the apartment."

"*Santa Maria.* No, that won't be necessary."

"One of the condoms must have failed. Or something. Maybe we were one of the victims of whoever has been going around stabbing holes in condom packages. I take it you didn't inspect it before using it."

No, he hadn't inspected it. At the time he'd just been happy that his memories would include safe sex.

Only no one who played with fire was ever truly safe. And Sara was fire. And, at the moment, ice.

"I'm pregnant. I'll do a test here at the hospital as well, if you want, but I really didn't come here to tell you that."

"Are you kidding me? The words 'I'm pregnant' just happened to fall out of your mouth and land on the floor?"

"Oh, I meant to say it. The other thing is this. I'm clean. I've only been with one other man in my life—and he didn't stick around for long."

The pain of those words tore at him, erasing some of his horror. But sticking around wasn't always the best thing that someone could do.

His father, for example.

Yeah, he'd stuck around, but he'd gotten some on the side as well.

She licked her lips. "Are you clean? If there's any doubt, I need to know now."

He laughed. As if dropping a bombshell like being pregnant wasn't enough, now she wanted to know if he'd shot anything besides his sperm into that condom? But if anyone should understand it should be him. In medical school they'd stressed that STDs needed to be reported and partners traced, if at all possible. Sara was trying to do the responsible thing.

So the pregnancy angle was just a little sidebar to the real issue? Would she have even told him about the baby if she hadn't been worried about whether or not he'd given her something?

He didn't even want to think about that.

But pregnant?

Dammit. Lightning really could strike twice. He'd been an unplanned child. And now he'd repeated history with Sara.

"I'm clean. I get tested once a year at the hospital because I work with immunocompromised individuals." He jerked his shoulder to the side to make it crack. The sharp sound was followed by a quick rush of endorphins. An old *futebol* injury had turned into a bad habit. One he couldn't seem to break.

"I should know that. Sorry."

His brain tried to make sense of things, but right now that subway train was rushing past at speeds that caused his head to swim. "You're sure. You're pregnant."

"Do you want to say it a couple more times?" She heaved in a deep breath and then let it out so fast that it sent tendrils of her hair flying to the sides. "Listen, I know this is a shock. It is to me too. But I couldn't live with myself if I didn't at least inform you."

"Inform me." His thoughts wavered. So she'd planned on telling him even without the STD angle. Although… "Are you thinking of terminating?"

"No! I wasn't. I'm not." She paused. "I'm sorry if that makes you unhappy. My dad once told me I was an unplanned pregnancy, and I ended up being the only child they could have. I just can't. I won't. So I'm asking you again. Do you want me to quit my job?"

His parents' bitter marriage came to the forefront of his mind. His folks had stayed together because of him and, later, Natália. They'd as much as admitted it on several occasions. He'd sworn that was never ever going to happen to him. And yet here stood a woman who told him she was expecting a child.

Because of him.

Suddenly he was faced with a horrible decision that really wasn't a decision at all. He knew what he had to do.

"No, Sara, I don't want you to quit. I…" Words suddenly rose up from the abyss, unbidden. Maybe it was an old protective streak left over from when his sister had been sick. Whatever it was, they tore out of his mouth before he could stop them. "I'll help support you. And the baby, of course."

Support her? As in with money?

Sara's chest burned as she stared at him in disbelief. Oh, hell, no.

"Are you kidding me, Sebastian? I don't want your money. I'm insulted you would even say that to me."

"Then why did you come? Do you want a proposal?"

The muscles in her abdomen tightened until she could barely breathe. "What is wrong with you? When I get married, it's going to be because I love someone. Not because I'm pregnant with his child."

A cord of tension appeared in his jaw.

"I'm trying my best to do the responsible thing here. If I fathered a child, I certainly want to help take care of it."

"If?" A chill went through her. "You did. And the responsible thing would be to sit down and calmly work through where we go from here, as far as this job goes. If my being here will make it too awkward for you, then I'll move back to Rio Grande do Sul."

And take the baby with her. She left the words unsaid, but they hung in the air nonetheless. Only it wasn't just her baby. It was his too. And her conscience wouldn't let her just keep working with him without telling him the truth. She could have. It would have been so easy. When her condition became evident, he would just assume that the baby was someone else's. He probably wouldn't even have asked. In the end, she couldn't bring herself to be that dishonest.

"Why even tell me? Why not just leave and not look back?"

"Is that what you wish I had done?"

He turned away, going to stand by a large window at the back of his office. From where she stood she could see several apartment buildings fanned out into the distance. A sky-high office with a gorgeous view. This man was so far out of her league it wasn't even funny.

And they'd made a baby together. Tears gathered behind her eyes.

"No. It isn't what I wish you'd done."

He wished it hadn't happened at all. He didn't say it, but he might as well have.

"Don't worry, I'm not asking for anything. I don't *want* anything. I just thought you deserved to know."

He turned around to face her, putting his hands on his desk and looking across it at her. "It's my child too, Sara. If you're keeping it, I'm serious. I'll assume responsibility for it." His cool clinical tone dashed away any urge to cry.

Her heart became a chunk of granite, continuing to pulse and push blood through her system but refusing to feel. "Please, don't think you have to do that. Lots of women raise children on their own. It happens all the time nowadays."

"It's my child too." The repeated phrase was a little softer this time. A little less clinical. "Don't try to keep me out of its life."

That took her aback. Far from telling her to get away from him or, worse, just throwing money at her to assuage his guilt, he was saying he wanted to be a part of the baby's life. Marriage or no marriage.

"No, of course not. I just assumed you wouldn't want anything to do with it."

He gave a rough snort. "You don't know me very well, then. I practically raised my little sister because our parents—let's just say they weren't exactly the doting type. My dad cheated, and Natália's cancer diagnosis ended up being the only glue that held them together."

That shocked her into silence for several seconds.

"I'm sorry. I had no idea." Why was he even telling her this? Her parents' marriage had been the exact opposite. They had loved her with an all-encompassing type of love. And they *were* the doting type. They doted on her. And on each other. She couldn't imagine anything sadder than to grow up in a home devoid of that kind of love.

Sara wasn't so sure her parents' kind of love existed any more. Her runaway boyfriend was a case in point.

"It's not something I talk a lot about. I'm not even sure why I told you, except to say that I don't want any child of mine to go through life not knowing that he or she is loved."

"He or she will be. By me. And by my father."

"But not by me, is that it?"

"I won't try to keep you out of his or her life." That would be making one mistake into an even bigger one. She just wanted to make sure that's what Sebastian wanted to do. She couldn't bear the thought of him being a part-time dad and then at some point down the road deciding it wasn't for him and walking out of his child's life. Like her boyfriend had done to her. No, if he was going to do that, he could just forget about it. "But think carefully about it. Because once you decide, there will be no going back. It wouldn't be fair to the baby."

"I don't need to think about it."

She shook her head, a steely determination she hadn't

known she possessed coming to the fore. Or maybe her maternal instincts were already kicking in. Whatever it was, she felt a fierce protective drive that wouldn't be denied. "Oh, but I insist. Take a couple of weeks. Or, better yet, a month. Think about it. Weigh the pros and cons of all that will be involved in a lifetime of parenting. And then get back to me with whatever you decide."

He came around the desk and took her by the shoulders. "I don't need a month, Sara. Or even a day. I am telling you right now. I want to be involved in this child's life."

"Are you sure?" Suddenly she was backpedaling like crazy.

They stared at each other for several seconds, and then Sebastian's grip softened, his gaze dropping to her mouth before coming back up.

"I've never been more sure of anything in my life."

A shiver went through her.

Céus! What did she think she was doing, handing down ultimatums? He was a city man, well versed in the comings and goings of relationships, just like her ex. To him, she probably seemed like a country bumpkin. And right now, unlike what she'd just told him, she did indeed want to go back in time. To six weeks ago and a certain wedding, actually. If she could, she might have made another choice. And she certainly would have brought her own damn protection.

Except what was done was done. Whether she liked it or not.

And now she was going to just have to stand back and accept the consequences.

Lucas Carvalho's clinic was in the heart of the Favela do São João. The addition of the tiny healthcare post had added a measure of hope to a desperate population. And, actually, Lucas had named the clinic to reflect that: The Star of Hope Clinic. Joined by Adam Cordeiro, Sebastian had driven here to meet up and get some inside information on the residents and hopefully figure out the biggest areas of need. Adam was already donating a couple of hours a week to the staffing of the clinic. They were scheduled to go out and get drinks together after the meeting.

To tell his friends or not to tell them. That was the question. He was still on shaky ground where Adam was concerned. His sister seemed happy, though, and that was all that mattered. Or it should be.

Adam parked the car in front of the whitewashed little building. The red dirt of the favela—splashed up by rainfall and street traffic—stained the bottom half of the clinic. Even so, with its flower-filled planters that hung beneath each window, the building was cleaner than most of the others in the neighborhood. The greenery and the cheery hand-lettered sign had to be the work of Lucas's wife.

Adam turned to him, pausing with his hand on the door latch. "Just so I'm sure, is everything okay between us?"

Sebastian had been silent for most of the trip from the hospital, and he knew he hadn't been acting quite like himself for the past several months. Time to make amends, if he could. "Yeah, it's all good. Sorry about being such an ass about everything."

"I would have wondered about you if you hadn't gotten in my face. I never saw myself as good enough for Natália."

"You're perfect for her." He sent his friend a forced

grin. "But I know where to find you if that silver perfection ever tarnishes."

"Not going to happen, bro. I'm pretty crazy about the woman. Someday you'll meet the right one and understand exactly what I'm talking about."

Hardly. But that made his decision. He wouldn't say anything about Sara's announcement. Not yet. Not until he absolutely had to. "Like you said, 'Not going to happen, bro.'"

Adam rolled his eyes and stepped out of the car. "I seem to remember saying almost the exact same thing. And now look at me."

Lucas met them at the door. Great. Another happily married friend to contend with.

And if Sara had said she wanted a proposal, would he have given her one? He didn't think so. It would have been for all the wrong reasons. Just like his parents.

"I heard you got Dona Talita worked into the schedule at Tres Corações," he said. "I appreciate that."

Lucas stood aside to let them through the door. "Not a problem. She'll have surgery in a couple of weeks and a follow-up with an endocrinologist to get her blood sugar level back on track. I appreciate you making her a priority. She wouldn't have gone on her own."

"Sara Moreira, the nurse working with me in the mobile clinic, had a lot to do with it."

"Well, whatever the reason, it's great news."

The inside of Lucas's clinic was just as simple as the outside. White plaster walls and white tiles were all easy to disinfect. The space had been divided into three small areas: a spartan waiting room with plastic chairs lining the walls, a small but efficient exam room, and a tiny office that he could see from the waiting area. It contained just a basic metal desk. From what he understood, Lucas took the laptop that held all his patient information with him when he left the building to keep anyone from having a reason to break in and steal anything. Actually, his friend had made it so there was very little to steal. Some cotton balls and tongue depressors maybe, but he kept most of his equipment in tubs that he loaded in and out of his van whenever he was here.

If only Sebastian could load and unload his problems like that. Just tuck them out of sight until he was ready to deal with them again. Only he didn't feel like he would ever be ready to deal with a certain unexpected "problem".

And he damned himself for even thinking of it as a problem. It just hadn't been planned, the way he liked to do with most of his life. A product of having to care for his sister and act as referee for his parents' arguments. He was an expert at compartmentalizing.

Only how did you compartmentalize a child?

Or his or her mother?

You didn't. At least not in a way he was accustomed to.

"Is the clinic open today?"

Lucas shook his head. "Not today. Sophia has finally convinced me that I need to take a day or two off each month to 'recharge my batteries', as she put it."

"A day or two a month? I should say so. That's where I come in, I assume."

"Yes, if you have time." He pulled three of the white chairs from their spots along the wall and dragged them to the center. He motioned them to sit. "Adam is already working two hours a week. I don't want you to feel like you need to be at the clinic itself, since I know you're going to be putting the hours in with the mobile clinic. If I could just plan it so that the clinic is closed on the day the mobile unit is here, that would be great. I can send you cases, if you want, like I did the last time."

"That works for me. In between patients, then, I could park by the clinic and if someone has a need they can just stop by. That way it'll be easy to find me."

Adam glanced his way. "Maybe you should have a key to the clinic and just meet patients in here?"

"I'd rather keep things as simple as possible, actually. I'll email you information on any patients I see, just like I did with my first two. It will make your record-keeping easier, I think. And I'll know where everything is inside the truck."

"How are things going with Sara, by the way?" Adam asked. "You two getting along? You seemed to be making eyes at each other at the wedding. Or was that just my imagination?"

Great, he'd been hoping no one had noticed.

"Your imagination. There were no 'eyes'. Or anything else involved. Sara and I have only been working together for a week. We'll see how it goes in a few more. But hopefully any possible issues have been resolved."

Except for one.

The bombshell she'd dropped earlier in the day still seemed unreal, like it had happened to a different Sebastian in an alternate universe. He didn't do things like get drunk and get women pregnant.

Only he hadn't set out to get her pregnant. Even drunk, a little part of his head had tried to do the right thing by protecting them both.

Instead, he'd failed.

Lucas glanced at him. "What issues?"

"Just a little lovers' spat." Adam said it with a grin, but the words hit Sebastian just the wrong way.

"We are not lovers." The words came out half growled.

"Whoa." Lucas's brows shot up. "I'm pretty sure Adam was kidding."

"Sorry." He popped his shoulder joint and sighed. "It's been stressful trying to get the hospital administration fully on board with the mobile unit. If you knew how many hoops I've had to jump through to get this up and running, you'd be buying me a drink—or five."

"If that's what you need, you got it." Adam slapped him on the back.

No, it wasn't what he needed. What he needed was a way out of his predicament. One that had both him and Sara coming out of it unscathed. Once she started showing, and people started asking questions…

Talk about hoops. Somehow he didn't think Paulo Celeste would approve of Sara suddenly expecting his child right after going to work for the hospital.

Dammit, he hadn't even thought about that. Until now. Surely it was no one's business.

But people were curious. They were bound to ask. And the truth would come out, even if he didn't want it to.

He hadn't technically broken hospital policy that he knew of, since Sara hadn't been working for the hospital when she'd gotten pregnant. And if he'd known about it before she'd come to Santa Coração, he would have vetoed them hiring her. But he hadn't known. Neither had she.

Or so she said. What if that's why she'd wanted to come to the hospital? Because she'd already known about the pregnancy?

No, she'd been genuinely shocked.

"Drinking's what got me into this mess."

"What mess?" Both men were now staring at him. It was then that he realized the words hadn't gone with the conversation at hand. Talk about letting the cat out of the bag. They were going to find out. Better that it came from him than from the hospital grapevine. And maybe they could give him some advice on how to handle things.

"Sara's pregnant."

"Sara?" Lucas frowned. "As in your new nurse, Sara?"

"Yep."

"Wow, she didn't reveal this at her interview? It's going to be pretty damned difficult to replace her, isn't it, when she goes on maternity leave? When is she due?"

Sebastian did some quick mental calculations and came up blank. "Subtract six weeks from nine months."

"Six weeks." Adam planted his elbows on his knees and leaned forward. "That's back when Natália and I got married, so let's see… Do not even tell me."

It was now or never. "I think I just did. We'd both had a little too much to drink and things got—out of control."

How lame did that sound?

Lucas's gaze sharpened. "*You're* the father?"

"It would seem that way."

Adam shook his head, patent disbelief on his face. "What was it you said to me in the car a few minutes ago? 'Not going to happen'?"

"It's not. We're not. It was an accident."

"Is she going to keep it?"

Lucas's question was innocent enough, but it raised the hair on the back of his neck. Hadn't he asked her the same thing, though?

"Yes, she's going to keep it."

"Well, congratulations. I think."

"Yes," said Adam. "Congratulations. Sometimes things don't go as planned. I'm proof positive of that. But they tend to work out the way they were supposed to."

Not for his mom and dad. Not for Natália either, in getting cancer. But there was no way he could say that.

"We'll see."

"Are you going to keep working with her?"

Sebastian gave a shrug. "What else can I do? If we tell anyone, things could get messy. Worst-case scenario is that she'd be asked to leave the project."

"Because of that? Even if she is, surely there are other jobs at the hospital."

"We're currently on a hiring freeze, according to the hospital administrator. Unless someone quits, we can't hire any additional personnel, because of the economy tanking. Sara was already the exception to the rule. I imagine the other local hospitals are in the same spot."

"I know Tres Corações is. Damn, that puts you in kind of a touchy situation, though, doesn't it?" Lucas propped a foot on his knee.

"Touchy is how he got into this."

"Oh, you're a funny, funny guy, Adam." He knew his friend was trying to lighten the atmosphere, but right now there was nothing anyone could say or do to make this any easier. In truth, Sebastian held both his future and Sara's in the palm of his hand. He'd spoken the truth. If he let Paulo know, the man might start worrying about corporate sponsors and turn sour on the whole Mãos Abertas project. Sara would probably then be let go because of a lack of other job positions, and Sebastian himself might receive an unwelcome lecture on maintaining professional appearances.

And with the mobile clinic being an experiment, he could very well sink its chances for continuing into the future. All because of a single error in judgment.

Sara was going to pay for it, and so was he. But he would be damned if all of the patients who'd stood to be helped by this endeavor would pay.

So he would just have to do his best to keep this thing under wraps. Starting with Adam and Lucas.

Then, he somehow had to convince Sara to keep her pregnancy a secret for the next several months. Or else ask her to go back to Rio Grande do Sul before anyone at the hospital got wind of the situation.

Even if she hated him for it.

CHAPTER FIVE

"I ALREADY TOLD YOU. I'm not planning on telling anyone. At least not right away."

When Sebastian had called her into his office this morning, she'd expected him to maybe try to get her to agree to let him support her again.

Not a chance. He'd obviously seen the error of his ways and had decided on a different tack. Just shove his future child under a rug to keep the scandal from messing with his stellar reputation.

She should be glad and take that as evidence that he'd never gotten anyone else pregnant. Until she'd come along.

Instead, an oppressive weight of exhaustion came over her. Probably due to the early changes in her body from her pregnancy. She thought of something.

"I won't deny this baby prenatal care. And I'm not sure how you can keep it a secret if I'm seeing an obstetrician."

The pencil he'd picked up from his desk tilted back and forth between his thumb and index finger, the speed increasing. "I'm not asking you to not get medical care, I just…" His glance went beyond her as if he was thinking things through.

So he hadn't thought about that angle either. "Natália is a neonatologist, maybe she can help."

"In other words, you're willing to share the news with your sister as long as it benefits you." Her voice was flat. So he could dictate who knew and who didn't? To hell with that.

He shifted in his chair, the pencil in his hand going still. "This situation isn't easy for anyone."

"'Anyone' being?"

"Why are you so angry?" The pencil dropped onto the desk.

"I'm not. You just went from not caring if anyone knew to keeping it a complete secret."

Up went his brows. "I never planned on sending out birth announcements, so I don't know where you got that idea."

He'd started out by asking to be a part of this child's life. If that wasn't sending out an announcement, she didn't know what was. Or had he forgotten about that?

Since she couldn't think of a witty response, she clamped her jaws shut and willed them to stay that way. He stared at her for a few seconds.

"Do you want to go home?"

"I'm not sick. At least, not at the moment." She'd felt a couple of twinges earlier, but a pack of *água e sal* crackers had taken care of that.

"I don't mean to your apartment here at the hospital. I'm talking about Rio Grande do Sul."

A ripple of fear went through her, and she pressed her spine against the back of her chair. "Are you threatening to fire me?"

"What?" His eyes shut for a moment, fingers going to the bridge of his nose and pinching. When he looked up again, his gaze had softened. "Hell, no. I'm not threatening you, Sara. The hospital has been cutting costs for a while. That means no extraneous personnel."

"But the mobile clinic…" Was he saying they'd decided to do away with her job?

"Is an experiment. It's not guaranteed to continue. If there is the slightest glitch along the way, they could scrap the entire project."

A glitch. As in her pregnancy. Oh, Lord. She put herself in Sebastian's shoes for a second. A new nurse was hired to work with the illustrious Dr. Texeira and came up pregnant with his child soon afterwards. At the very least it would raise some eyebrows. Not many hospitals would tolerate questionable behavior on the part of its staff, especially if it affected its reputation. Even if the hospital wasn't affected, Sebastian could be. Especially if the news came out at just the wrong moment.

"I'm so sorry, Sebastian. I swear I didn't know about the pregnancy before I got here, or I never would have come."

"I believe you. The timing just—"

"Sucks."

One side of his mouth went up. "That's one way of putting it."

"I don't want them to squash the project." Which was a surprise, because a few days ago she had been wondering if she could even do this job. And then she'd seen what had happened with Talita Moises. Without the mobile clinic, she might never have sought treatment. And she probably would have died of an infection, somewhere down the road. Yet now she had a good chance of survival.

All because of the clinic.

"I don't either. But you're right. It's not worth risking your health or that of the baby." His fingers sought out the pencil again. "I'm sorry to say that Adam Cordeiro and Lucas, the doctor who runs the favela clinic, already know. It came out during a meeting. They won't say anything, but the wider the circle gets of those who know—and they will know—the harder it will be. Natália has to know at the very least. Any pharmacist who fills a prescription will know. Ultrasound technicians. The list goes on and on."

"I'll move to another hospital."

He shook his head. "As big as São Paulo is, most of the doctors know each other, and the pool of hospital administrators is even smaller."

"So what do you want me to do? Do you *want* me to go home?"

She couldn't believe she had even asked that question. It might be the easiest solution, but it wasn't what she wanted in her heart of hearts.

"Not unless that's what you want."

She leaned forward and put one of her hands on his desk. "I don't. I really think I could do some good here."

"I think you could too. I'm toying with an idea, but you probably aren't going to like it."

"I don't understand."

"I asked you if you expected a proposal when you first told me. A question to which I got a resounding no." He covered her hand with his own. "But think about it in the bright light of day, Sara. It's the perfect solution. There are several husband and wife teams that work at the hospital. If we did it quietly, and I told the hospital administrator that we had already been 'involved' before you came up here, no one would be the wiser. It would be the truth, to a certain extent."

She swallowed, finally understanding. "You want to get married. Why not just tell the administrator I'm pregnant? Surely this has happened before."

"Maybe. The administrator stressed that things needed

to stay professional between us. And since you're here doing a temporary *estágio*, it may be misconstrued as my taking advantage of my position."

"But you didn't. There has to be some way to explain all of this."

"If you can think of something, I'm all ears."

She racked her brain, but came up empty.

Sebastian squeezed her hand. "If you really want to stay here, I think it's what's best for the patients."

"So you'll make a noble sacrifice."

"No. I've never claimed to be noble." He blew out a breath. "I'm trying to help. To figure out a way that not only keeps the Mãos Abertos program up and running but also keeps you from losing your job."

"I'll go work at another hospital in the area."

"I already checked. The answers were all the same. No one is hiring. A lot of the health-care sector is operating in the red, and that situation doesn't look like it's going to improve anytime soon."

He'd already checked. Had already thought of sending her away to a different hospital to save his own ass?

No, he'd said it was to keep her from being sent home. She could only imagine what her dad would say. Actually, knowing her father, he'd probably travel up to São Paulo and give Sebastian a piece of his mind—if not worse. She'd been planning on keeping the baby a secret from him, at least for a while, so why was it any different that Sebastian wanted to keep the situation quiet?

It wasn't any different. It just hurt that he didn't trust her not to say anything. Realistically, though, if she stayed the whole six months, she was eventually going to show—and the secret would be out. And he was right about the list of people who would know once she started prenatal care.

But to get married because of it?

"I can't see myself marrying someone I don't love."

"And rightly so. I've seen where that can lead and it's not pretty. This would just be temporary. For maybe a year or two until well after the baby is born and your *estágio* is over. Then we get a quiet divorce. Just like lots of other couples."

Did he even hear himself? Her parents had been married for a long, long time, and they'd been happy. It was what she'd once hoped for herself. So to go through a sham of a marriage seemed disrespectful to her mom's memory somehow. And yet what else could she do? Abortion wasn't common in Brazil, but even if it was, she wouldn't choose that route. She wanted this baby.

There were several other married couples, he'd said—some of them probably had children—so they would just blend in with the crowd, was that it?

Maybe he was right.

He'd said it himself, this wouldn't be forever. And she certainly didn't have a boyfriend any more or even a distant prospect that could give her the cover story Sebastian wanted her to have.

"A year or two is kind of ambiguous. If I agree to this—and I haven't said I would—I would want to have a definite time frame so there are no misunderstandings on either side." Not that she expected Sebastian to fall head over heels for her and refuse to give her a divorce. No, it was more as a reminder to herself that he wasn't promising her roses and forever.

Sebastian's head cocked to the side. "How about we split the difference and say eighteen months, then? Can you stand to carry my name for that long?"

"Our situation wouldn't be any different than it is now,

would it? Just a fake marriage to keep our situation from ruining everything."

"The marriage would have to be legal, that's the only way any of this will work." He frowned. "And the situation wouldn't be any different, but your living arrangements would."

"I'm sorry?"

"Don't you think it would look kind of odd for a married couple to live in separate apartments?"

"I'm not sure… You want me to move in with you?" Surely that wasn't what he was saying.

"My apartment is big. You would practically have your own place with a few minor adjustments."

"How minor?" She was rapidly losing control of the situation. Was she actually thinking of going through with this? Of marrying a man who was practically a stranger?

Her mouth twisted. That certainly hadn't stopped her from sleeping with him. From carrying his child.

He'd said he wanted to be involved in the baby's life. What better way than to have said baby living under his roof for a few months after it was born? Except her *estágio* was only listed as being for six months. Was he inviting her to stay past that date? Maybe it was better not to ask.

"There are two bedrooms." He paused. "They share a bathroom, though. There's another one down the hall, but it's not a full bath. We'd have to work out a schedule for showering."

A shared bathroom. She could only imagine hearing the water running in there as he took his shower and picturing him naked. With water streaming down his…

She gulped. That was no minor adjustment. She would

have to invest in earplugs. Or something. "There are locks on the doors, right?"

Up went his brows. "Afraid I might try to sneak into your room while you're asleep?"

The thought of that made something in her tummy shift sideways. She covered it with a laugh.

"Of course not! I just don't want to walk in on you when you're in the bathroom."

"Yes, there are locks, Sara. Strong enough to keep out even the big bad wolf."

He might have meant it as a joke, but his words hit far too close to home for comfort. Because in that particular story the big bad wolf only wanted one thing. To devour Little Red Riding Hood. And he would do anything it took to get her.

Only Sebastian didn't want her. Not really. He just wanted to make sure his clinic stayed in business. And that she wasn't sent packing—although that was probably all part and parcel of making sure his pet project continued operating. Either way, she should be grateful. And she was. He was risking an awful lot for her. The least she could do was listen to his proposal and give him an honest answer.

"Tell me exactly how you expect all of this to work."

A week after making his crazy, impulsive suggestion, Sebastian found himself in a courthouse, reciting words that meant absolutely nothing to him. Worse, he was promising that he would keep to those words. Natália was there as a witness, although she had tried to talk him out of it several times. "This is too fast, Sebastian. It doesn't feel right."

It didn't feel right to him either. But once he'd decided, and Sara had agreed, there was nothing left but to go through with his scheme. As stupid as it now seemed.

Sara had asked that her father remain out of the loop. At least for a while. Once she got through her first trimester, when most miscarriages happened, she would tell him. As if getting married in secret would go over any better with him than it had with Natália.

This was seeming less and less like a good idea and more like a recipe for disaster.

Unless they could keep it together and do exactly what he'd said they would do: stay together until the baby was born and then for nine more months after that. When he broke it down like that, it didn't seem like such an eternity.

Who was he kidding? It already seemed like an eternity.

Wasn't it a small price to pay, though, to continue saving lives in the *favelas*?

Sara took the ring from his sister with a smile that wavered just slightly. That was okay, because everything inside him was wavering. And not just slightly, either.

Taking his hand in hers, she slid the thin band onto his ring finger. The ring he'd placed on hers moments earlier glittered an accusation at him. What would his child think of this once he or she was old enough to understand?

The same thing he'd thought when he'd found out the truth about his parents' marriage.

Hopefully he and Sara would exit this arrangement as friends, if nothing more. That was more than he could say for his mom and dad.

He glanced at Sara's face as she parroted the words the justice of the peace spoke. Her eyes were somber and unhappy.

Hell, he had practically forced her into doing this. He should have just asked her to go home. Oh, he'd blathered on about the project and it being canceled—and that was important. It was. But he'd also realized that if she left, he might never even see his child. There'd be no reason for her to seek him out. Especially if he'd sent her packing back to Rio Grande do Sul. And that killed him.

She took a breath, hesitating just a brief second longer than necessary. Sebastian gave her hand what he hoped was a reassuring squeeze, since he couldn't ask her if she was okay.

She did look at him then and returned the pressure.

A sense of relief went through him. He wasn't quite sure why—maybe he'd needed a little reassurance himself.

Then the stranger pronounced them husband and wife, inviting Sebastian to kiss his new bride. Natália glanced at him, brows raised in challenge. Fine. She thought it was too fast? That he was having second thoughts? He'd show both her and that smug official.

Cupping Sara's face in his hands and registering her slight gasp of shock as he did so, he lowered his head and planted his lips on hers. Only her mouth was a little sweeter than he remembered. A little more pliable. A lot more, in fact. If he hadn't known better, he might almost believe she was…

Returning his kiss.

He blinked, pulling back in an instant—somehow managing to fake a smile as he leaned down again and kissed the tip of her nose. There. Playful. That's how he would get through all of this. She was the mother of his child, but she was not his lover. He could treat her like a distant relative or a…

His glance went to Natália and a rock dropped to the

pit of his stomach. No, what he felt for Sara was nothing like the easy affection he held for his baby sister. It was more like the uneasy yearning that happened when he was around his mother and father. A wish for things to be different. Not good.

Natália came over and hugged his new wife, while sending him another silent glare over her shoulder. She mouthed, "This is wrong." Then she turned around and left the room. Well, there was nothing keeping her. She'd already signed the document that made all this legal.

But legal didn't necessarily make it right.

His plan was to talk to the hospital administrator as soon as they moved Sara into his house. He wasn't quite sure what his angle was going to be yet, because the man would undoubtedly ask if this was why he'd been so eager to start the project.

And then Sebastian would remind him that he'd been pushing for a mobile unit for the last two years. And it only made sense that he'd want to share something that was so important to him with those he loved.

Loved. That was a laugh.

The justice of the peace shifted, maybe sensing that the atmosphere in the room was darker than it should have been.

Sara saved him from trying to make small talk by glancing up at him. "You ready to head out?"

"Yes." He thanked the government official, and they walked out the door and into the blinding light of midday. He held a hand over his brow to shade his eyes, looking for his car. "That wasn't as bad as I thought it would be."

"Wasn't it?"

Sara's voice had a sad quality to it that he didn't like. Had he really done the right thing? Natália didn't think so.

"Hey." He took her hand and stopped her. "It's going to

be all right. Eighteen months will go by fast. And you'll have the baby to worry about soon enough."

"I know. It just seems dishonest somehow."

She and Natália were evidently reading from the same play book.

"Not dishonest. Just necessary."

The glare from the sun kept him from seeing her expression.

"Do you really think the administrator is going to buy our story?"

"He should, if we put on a united front. I'm pretty sure he's not going to fire one of the hospital's two oncological surgeons." He hesitated. "Would you be willing to roll part of your salary into mine? I can make up the difference. But if Paulo Celeste thinks he stands to gain something from the arrangement, he'll be much more likely to overlook any slivers of doubt. I'll talk to him."

She blinked. "Shouldn't that be 'we'?"

"I think it will be easier if I do it alone."

Pulling her hand away, she shook her head. "It's my life too. You talked about presenting a united front. How can we do that if I'm not even there?"

"He's been known to yell." Something that always made Sebastian distinctly uncomfortable, since his parents did that routinely.

"I'm a big girl. I think I can handle it."

She might be able to, but could he?

"If you're sure, I won't try to stop you."

He saw a flash of something that could have been teeth. "You can ask my father how easy it is to stop me once I have my mind set on something."

"That bad, huh?"

"The worst. He says I'm more stubborn than a steer during cutting and branding season."

"I have no idea what that even means."

She tilted her head and gave him a look. "No? Where I'm from, everyone knows what that means. I'm sure you city guys have a similar expression."

"Not really." Especially not since that sassy little look she'd just sent him had arrowed straight down to his groin. Probably remembering that kiss a few moments earlier.

"Sure you do. 'More stubborn than...'" She gave a little hand flourish that told him to fill in the blank.

Cornered, he forced his sluggish brain to think of something. Anything. "More stubborn than a V-fib that refuses to be converted."

"Okay, I'm not sure I like being compared to a deadly arrhythmia."

She was right. It was a stupid comparison. And a stupid game.

"Let's just go get your stuff and move it over to my apartment. And then tomorrow we'll tackle telling the hospital administrator."

"Are you sure you don't want to wait a few weeks? Until we see if the pregnancy is even viable?"

"Someone is bound to mention you moving out of the hospital apartments. And then it will be harder to explain away."

"I guess you're right. I just hate lying to people."

"Let's just concentrate on what's true, okay? It's true that we got married, is it not?" He turned and started walking back toward the car.

"Yes."

"It's true that you're moving into my place, right?"

"Um—yes." She caught up to him a few yards later. "But we don't love each other."

"When was the last time you asked a newly married couple if they loved each other?"

"Well...never."

He unlocked the passenger side door and waited until she climbed inside. "That's right, because you just assume they got married because they fell in love. The hospital administrator will assume the same thing. I doubt he'll even ask."

"I hope you're right."

"Don't worry. As soon as I mention combining incomes, the dollar signs in his eyes will block out any objections he may have. He might even be happy for us." Sebastian carefully omitted the fact that he planned on making up the difference in her salary and putting it aside in a special account. And if she was able to carry the pregnancy to term, he would sock money away into a college fund. That news could wait until they started their divorce proceedings, though.

"And if it doesn't?"

"Then we'd better have an alternate explanation ready."

All he had to do was think of one. Between now and tomorrow morning.

CHAPTER SIX

Nossa! SARA COULD see why the condominium building was called the Vista do Vale, because the scenery from the twenty-fifth-floor balcony was spectacular. Sara had never been inside an apartment this luxurious. It certainly didn't feel like it was situated in a valley from where she was looking. After living her entire life in her parent's one-story house on the ranch, she felt kind of queasy about how high up they were. Or maybe that was her pregnancy. Honestly, it was probably a little bit of both.

"Where did you say the fire escape was?" She called back to where Sebastian was setting her two large suitcases on the polished marble floor of the foyer.

He came through the double sliding glass doors that opened to an outside living space. A space that was almost as big as her whole nurse's apartment at the hospital.

"I didn't, but see that platform hanging over there?"

"Where—? Oh, no!" She'd noticed the contraption hanging a few floors below them. Panic went through her system, the queasiness growing exponentially.

"Relax, Sara. I'm kidding. They're in the process of polishing and repairing the tile on this side of the building."

"In that?" No one in their right mind would stand on what appeared little more than a wooden platform with a thin line of metal railing encircling the outside. Even as she looked, it seemed to sway in the breeze. Her nausea spiked. There was no way she would go out in something like that.

She could tell the difference, though, in the cobalt tiles that had been polished and those that had collected years of dust and grime from the city below. Even the "before" view, though, oozed opulence and wealth.

"The company has many years of experience in this work. They know what they're doing."

She glanced down again, and then backed away, only to bump into Sebastian, whose arm went around her to brace her. The warmth of his touch soothed her rapidly fraying nerves. "Seriously, we could get out if there were a fire, right?"

"There are stairs, in case the elevator goes out."

"Have you ever had to use them?"

"I have. More than once."

"Deus do céu." She pressed both palms against her stomach. "Why?"

He turned her around to face him, hands still on her shoulders. "Hey, are you okay?"

"I think so. I just didn't think this would all be so…" She couldn't find the right word, so she settled for waving her hand to encompass the inside of his condominium. "How long have you lived here?"

"Not long. I moved here about a year ago."

"And you've already used the stairs more than once?"

His thumbs trailed over her collarbones as he peered into her face, as if seeing something that worried him. "I was kidding. I only went up and down them for exercise when I knew I wouldn't have time to go to the gym."

Her whole body sagged closer to him. "Well, you could have said that right away."

"I had no idea you were afraid of heights."

"I've never really had a chance to test out whether I was or wasn't. I think the tallest place I've ever been was the waterfall at Iguaçu."

"You really only notice the height out here. Inside, it just feels like a regular living space."

Regular living space? Was he kidding? There was nothing "regular" about his apartment. "I'll take your word for it." As much as she tried to keep her voice neutral, even she could hear the ironic overtones behind her comment. Besides, that continued brushing movement of his thumbs was beginning to warm her up in ways that worried her.

Maybe he read her thoughts, because he grinned and put his hand under her elbow. "Come on back inside, and I'll show you where you'll be staying. Since you're such a fan of heights, maybe I'll take you to the observation deck of the Banespa building. You can see a lot of the heart of the downtown area from there. You can even see this building from it."

Groaning, she let him lead her back inside. "Are there stairs there too?" She could see this being a common litany for her time in São Paulo.

"There are, but we'll want to take the elevator. Once we reach the thirty-third floor, we'll have to go up two flights of stairs to get to the deck."

Okay, so the fear was still there, but there was also a glimmer of excitement. Maybe it was from the gentle way he'd calmed her fears out on the veranda. Or because he wanted to take her to see parts of the city.

He's probably joking, Sara. You don't need to take any of this too seriously.

Because doing that could make for a whole lot of heartache. Especially since her wonky hormones were making her feel a little off—a touch lovey-dovey about everything—as it nurtured those maternal instincts. She had to remember that none of her emotions were trust-worthy at the moment. And Sebastian would be horrified if he thought she was looking down the road and pictur-ing them as an old married couple.

Not that she was. Even if the way he'd looked at her a few minutes ago had made her want things she couldn't have.

Good thing they had set up some ground rules.

"Well, we'll see. With the mobile clinic and your reg-ular rounds at the hospital, you'll probably be too busy to do much of anything outside of work."

"We have to eat lunch or dinner sometime." He threw a glance over his shoulder as he headed toward the foyer.

"We?"

"We'll be working most of the same hours, and we're newlyweds, remember? It stands to reason that we would want to eat together from time to time. Like Adam and Natália do. Or the other married couples who work at the hospital."

"The two couples who were at your sister's wedding. They both work at the hospital as well?"

"Kind of. Marcos does, as you know. You'll be seeing a lot of him around the oncology department. And his wife, Maggie, works there as well. Lucas and Sophia do quite a bit of relief work in poorer parts of the country, and of course Lucas runs the clinic in the *favela* we were at the other day. But, yes, it seems that Santa Coração is a breeding ground for romance, my sister included."

Okay, so if he had caught the irony in her earlier words, she had definitely caught a hint of sardonic deri-sion in his tone.

"You disagree with people falling in love?"

"I don't disagree with their decisions. I'm just saying that I tend to be a little more skeptical. I've witnessed some train-wreck marriages that never should have taken place."

Was he talking about theirs? This whole sham had been his idea, not hers. Maybe he was already regretting having suggested it. Or warning her not to get too attached. He needn't bother. Maybe she should try to reassure him on that point.

"Train wrecks have to be lifted off the tracks at some point. They're not permanent."

"Sometimes there are extenuating circumstances for them to linger." He reached down and picked up her luggage, no longer looking at her.

Oh, God. He *was* talking about them—about her pregnancy. Maybe she should have insisted on a prenup to make him feel better about everything. And here she was acting like a starstruck teenager about his apartment and the city in general. No wonder he was nervous.

"Hey." She caught at his arm, the biceps tightening beneath her touch. "Stop for just a minute, please."

Sebastian set her luggage down and turned to face her, his eyes a dark molten mass of—anger? "What is it?"

She took her hand off him in a hurry.

"If you're worried about me trying to extend our arrangement, don't. I'll sign a prenup or a contract, if you want. It's not too late for either."

"What are you talking about?"

She shrugged, needing to look away from those huge pupils. "I'm talking about this farce. I didn't want to do it in the first place, remember, and I only agreed in order to—"

"No. I'm sorry." His hands went to her shoulders once again, gaze softening. "I wasn't referring to you at all.

I know you didn't try to trap, coerce or whatever other words you think are rattling around in my head right now. I'm talking about my folks. They haven't been the greatest example of marital bliss. Natália and I both know they stayed together for our sake. And now they just—stay together, probably because they've been married for so long. But they're not happy. I don't remember them *ever* being happy."

"How awful." She tried to switch gears, but all she felt was a huge sense of relief, mixed with sadness. "Surely they must love each other. Some couples just show it differently." Her dad was a good example of that. He had always been a man of few words, but he had loved his wife deeply. So deeply she didn't know if he would ever marry again.

"I don't think the word 'divorce' is used as a weapon in most homes. I was surprised when Natália decided to get married at all. Especially as quick as it was."

"They seem very happy. At least from what little I've seen. Natália and I are friends. Surely she would have mentioned something if there was trouble in paradise."

"I'm sure they're fine. I just wonder how long it can— Forget it. I shouldn't have mentioned any of it."

She reached up and covered one of his hands with her own. "Yes, you should have. It helps me understand how hard this whole situation is for you. But we don't hate each other. At least, I don't hate you."

One side of his mouth went up and his fingers tightened their grip on her shoulders before he let go of one and caught her hand. "You probably should. I keep telling myself I should have checked those condoms when I put them on, but I wasn't quite myself that night."

"Neither of us were. Knowing about your parents helps

me understand. And I don't hate you. I hope we'll come out of this as friends."

"Hmm—friends." His smile slid just a bit higher. "That can be a loaded term. My sister and Adam started out as friends. Look what happened with them."

This time he was joking. She should be elated that they'd gotten everything out in the open, but there was this vague sense of loneliness rolling around inside her. "Not all friends become lovers."

His thumb stroked over the palm of her hand, sending a shiver through her.

Careful, Sara.

"No, they don't. But former lovers can become friends, don't you think? We just have to make sure we don't go on any more drinking binges."

They were in trouble, then, because the low thrum of his voice was as intoxicating as any liquor. And his thumb, still scrubbing across her palm in a soft back and forth motion, was making her nerve endings tingle in spots far removed from her hand. Was he doing that on purpose? If so, she should tell him to stop. Except it felt good. Intimate in a way that rough, grabbing hands could never be.

"Well, since I'm not allowed to drink until after the baby is born, there's nothing for either of us to worry about."

Right?

"Nothing at all." Sebastian's voice deepened, laced with a tension she hadn't heard since—

That night at the bar. Right before he'd swept her off to that motel.

Deus! It had to be her imagination. She was letting it run wild. If she just tugged her hand, he would release her and all would be right with the world.

But even though her brain tried to tell her arm to slide backward, it stayed right where it was.

Okay, Sara, try something else. Hurry!

Before she could, his mouth kicked up sideways in a half-smile that drove the wind from her lungs.

"Do you do that on purpose?" He let go of her hand, his index finger traveling up to her lower lip and making it wiggle slightly. The touch went through her like an electric shock. It took her a second to find enough words to answer.

"Do what?"

"Puff that out when you're nervous about something." He let his hand drop back to his side, although his gaze stayed put.

She sucked the errant lip back over her teeth before realizing how ridiculous that was. "No. At least I don't think I do."

"I noticed it for the first time at the wedding."

He had? Her insides quivered with heat. Was he doing *that* on purpose?

She tried to clear her throat, but it came out as a weak puff of air that sounded more like a sigh. Maybe because that's what it was. Time to change the subject. "You were going to show me the bedrooms?"

No, wait. That huskiness in her voice wasn't right. And that low pulsing in her belly—the one telling her to do strange things—had to belong to someone else.

"You lip is doing that thing again." He shifted closer. "And there is nothing I would like better than to show you the bedrooms. Except for maybe—this."

His head lowered until he was hovering just above her mouth. *"Posso?"*

Deus. Did he have to ask?

"Yes." She drew the word out, letting that *s* roll across

her tongue, everything inside her screaming for him to close the gap between them and kiss her.

Then he was right there, his hand moving to cup her chin. This was no tentative, questioning touch. It was mouth to mouth and beyond, a display that said this had been just as much on his mind as it had been on hers.

She opened to him, shuddering when his tongue slid easily inside, his exploration turning into long, lazy movements that left no doubt as to where his thoughts were. *Graças a Deus*, that was a relief, because hers were in exactly the same place.

His arm went around her waist, hauling her against him, widening his stance so she fit between his legs. And, yes, that hard ridge of flesh was right where she expected it to be: cradled in the soft flesh of her belly.

The bedrooms. His. Hers. She didn't care which, but she needed to be there. But to say anything, she would have to pull her mouth away from the sweet thrill of having him inside. And she wasn't willing to forgo that. Not yet. In fact, she closed her lips around him, relishing the groan that followed soon afterwards.

He wheeled back in a rush, separating himself so quickly that she just stood there dazed for a second.

What? No!

Just when she thought he had come to his senses, he reached down, his arm going behind her knees and scooping her feet out from under her. He gave her a little toss to settle her against his chest, leaving her to clutch at his shoulders. "Do you still want to see where I sleep?"

All she could do was give a single nod that had him striding down the hallway, past one closed door and stopping in front of another.

She licked her lips, his taste still as fresh as it had been seconds earlier. When he made no move to go inside, she asked, "Do you need me to get the door?"

"Mmm…" He leaned down and kissed her again. "No, just anticipating what's going to happen once it's open."

He wasn't the only one. But she was getting impatient, and a little afraid he might back out at the last second.

She unhooked one of her arms and reached toward the ornate silver lever, her fingers barely able to brush against it. Sebastian obliged by tipping her far enough so she could grab it. She pushed down, the latch releasing and allowing the door to swing in.

"Waiting is highly overrated."

He gave her a heated glance, chuckling. "Oh, but the pleasure is that much sharper when it finally arrives."

The words made her shiver. Did that mean he meant to draw this out?

He moved inside the room and set her on the edge of a huge bed, his presence preventing her from closing her legs. That was okay, because the way he was standing was pure invitation. All she had to do was…

She scooted closer, fingers sliding up his thighs only to have his hands grab both of hers.

"What are you doing, Sara?"

"Didn't they teach you anything in sex education class?" She gave him what she hoped was a sexy grin.

"Oh, I have plenty of education. Want to see?"

He spread her hands so they were wide apart and then bore her back onto the bed. His kiss was immediate. Almost aggressive. And her hips arched high, trying to find him.

He lifted his head to look at her. "Since you don't seem interested in slow and easy, let's go fast and hard, shall we?"

One leg spread hers even further, settling his length in the opening he'd created.

"Yes!" This time when her hips went up, they connected with him, a jolt of sensation careening through her. She repeated the movement, her pleasure centers engaging in an instant. Okay, this was good. A little too good. On her third foray around the sun she slid along him, eyes fluttering closed as she ventured closer to—

He edged away. "I changed my mind."

"What?" Her eyes snapped open.

Her reaction was met with a rough laugh. "Just kidding. Let me get my zipper down, okay?"

She sucked down a relieved breath. "No protection needed tonight."

"Oh, no? I think you might need a little."

She tried to figure out what he meant, but her brain was too clouded with wanting him. "A little what?"

"A little protection. From me."

Evidently he'd gotten his zipper down because his fingers were at the top of her waistband, undoing the button and sliding the fastener. But when he went to tug her pants down, he could only get them past her hips. Her spread legs prevented them from going any lower. "Won't. Work."

He leaned down and bit her neck. "Want to bet?"

"No. A bet isn't what I want right now."

"I think I know exactly what you want." He pushed her legs together and then hauled her pants and underwear off. Then he was back again.

Up went her hips, just like before, seeking him.

This time, he found her instead and plunged home in a rush that drove the breath from his lungs. Sweet, sweet heat gripped him, massaging the ache right out of his flesh and replacing it with a need to drive into her again and again.

Forcing himself to count to ten, he only made it to five before those sexy hips were at it once more, trying to locate the very relief he'd been hoping to delay.

Damn, he hadn't even gotten her shirt off. And maybe they wouldn't make it that far, because his muscles were starting to take on a life of their own, her movements coaxing an equal and opposite reaction from him.

Soon the pace quickened, the thrusts growing quicker, getting wilder. Her head tossed from side to side as he hovered over her, his elbows braced on either side of her arms. Then he dove deep. Stayed there.

Her grip on him tightened. Squeezed.

Deus do céu. He wasn't going to be able to hold on much longer.

Her hips suddenly bucked up and back, her hands going to his butt, nails digging in. The sharp pain sent him over the edge, but not before he felt that blessed series of spasms that signaled her orgasm. That was it, he was off like a shot, pumping like a wild beast, his body erupting right along with hers.

He kept that ecstasy going as long as he could, until gravity stuck suckered tentacles on his flesh and began to drag him back to earth. He tried to resist, because he knew as soon as he landed, his first thought was going to be—

He hit with a bump.

And there it was. That raging, damning thought that happened every time he was around her:

How in the hell could he have let that happen?

CHAPTER SEVEN

"YOU'RE MARRIED? CONGRATULATIONS." The hospital administrator barely looked up from his papers.

Okay, so this wasn't the reception he'd expected. No conflict of interest speeches or comments about there needing to be oversights.

Maybe finding out that Sara was pregnant wouldn't have been such a big deal either. Although the administrator had been known to come down on anyone who might give the gossip columns something to chew on. Some of their more conservative sponsors were pretty strict about the hospital's reputation. That included its staff.

Paulo was all about keeping things running as smoothly as possible and making sure the income and expenses were lined up in neat little rows. Sponsors and benefactors had to be kept happy.

"As of two days ago, yes." He didn't even want to think about what they'd done on their honeymoon night. In fact, that was why he was here alone, instead of presenting that united front they'd talked about. He hadn't been able to face her at the apartment. Not yet.

He'd been pretty careful to come home when Sara was already in bed and leave before she got up in the morning. That had meant taking naps in his office during the day, but it was the only way he could function.

"Good, good. Make sure the nurses' housing department knows that there's an empty apartment available. And make sure Human Resources knows about her name change for tax purposes."

Name change. He'd forgotten about that. Damn.

"Right, I will." The sooner he got out of this office the better. He was going to have to tell Sara that it went well, but maybe he wouldn't let on just how well it had gone. "Thank you."

The man waved him away, before looking up suddenly. Sebastian tensed, waiting for the ax to finally fall.

"If you could write me up a statement on how things are going with the mobile clinic, I would like to use it for publicity. Maybe along with a congratulations announcement and a picture of the happy couple. We've had a couple of weddings over the last year or so. It might make for some good visibility for the hospital."

What the hell? Oh, Sara would just love that. And the man would probably get a big kick out of knowing they hadn't really spoken much over the last couple of days. Just some business stuff. But that would change tomorrow when they had to meet to do their rounds in the *favela*. There was no way to maintain silence when you were trapped together in a vehicle for an entire day.

"I'll check with her and see what she thinks."

The man's eyes narrowed slightly. "I would think that as a new hospital employee, she would be glad to help in any way she could."

A veiled threat? Not happening. And Sebastian wasn't about to let it slide by unnoticed.

"Would you care to rephrase that, sir?" The hospital might think it could do without Sara, but could it do without both of them? There were only a handful of on-cologists that could do what he did in the field of osteo-sarcoma.

"I stated that badly. You're right. Ask her if she would be willing to be photographed with you for hospital pub-licity. We're asking our other married couples to do the same for our Valentine's Day campaign. If she'd rather not, I won't push it."

"Thank you. I'll ask her and get back to you."

With that he headed out the door.

Only to barely miss crashing into Adam.

He matched his step to his friend's. "Did Paulo Celeste try to talk you and Nata into doing pictures for some kind of wedded bliss publicity stunt?"

"Yep, he's hoping to feature all the couples in the hospital for a Dia dos Namorados ad. Why? Did he say something to you about it?"

Okay, so Paulo had been telling the truth, it wasn't just him and Sara. He could understand that since Brazil's version of Valentine's Day would be here in a few months.

"Yes, he asked if Sara and I would pose next to the mobile clinic."

"Ironic, isn't it?" His friend shot him a glance.

"What do you mean?"

"Just that after all the objections you had about me and Nata, you end up married a month and a half later. Your sister has a few reservations about how it all went down."

He gave Adam a half-grin. "I would tell you to mind your own business, but since that seemed to be your line several months ago, I won't bother."

"Yeah, and somehow the request never made any dif-ference, no matter how nicely I asked."

He laughed. "Nicely? I remember some pretty heated moments there toward the end."

"And who started those moments?" Adam stopped at the bank of elevators and pushed a number into the console, waiting to see which elevator assignment came up on the screen.

"I'm not afraid to admit it." He slapped his friend on the back. "I'm also not afraid to admit when I was wrong about something. Natália seems happy. Really happy. I'm glad for both of you."

"Thanks. And you, Sebastian. Are you happy?" The letter E pinged on the screen. "Don't answer that. Just know that I want the same for you as what Nata and I have."

As his friend went over to Elevator E, Sebastian sighed. Some people didn't find happiness as easily as others. He'd already resigned himself to that fate. And since history seemed to like repeating itself, he knew better than to hope that it might get any better. His best bet was to hope it didn't get any worse.

It was worse. Sara barely said a word to him when she met him by the mobile clinic the next day. He couldn't blame her. He'd avoided her for the last three days. Mainly because he didn't have a clue what to say to make things better. He'd promised himself—and her—that it was a marriage on paper only. He'd even assured her there were locks on the doors, because she hadn't trusted him to keep his hands to himself. And rightly so. Less than an hour after they'd arrived in his home, he'd been all over her.

Was that what his father had been like as he'd had affair after affair—allowing his baser instincts to run the show? Wasn't that what had gotten Sebastian into this quandary in the first place?

Droga!

He paused before starting the vehicle, even though the heat was beginning to cause perspiration to bead on his forehead. "Sara?"

"Hmm?" She stared out the window as if something out there fascinated her. Since all that was there was a bunch of parked cars, he was pretty sure she was just avoiding interacting with him. He couldn't blame her.

"I think we need to at least try to get past this."

This time she did glance his way. But only for a second. "Past what?"

Was she kidding him? "What happened the other night."

"I'm already past it. Way past."

Great. He hadn't been able to work his way through things, and yet she acted like it hadn't meant any more than... Maybe she was too worried about something else. The baby?

"Are you feeling okay? Not sick?"

"Not today."

Okay, he was a first-class jerk. He'd been worried about his own comfort, while Sara was probably downing crackers by the dozen. "Morning sickness?"

"Not today."

"Well, then, when? Yesterday, dammit?" A flash of irritation went through him. He was just trying to help—to fix whatever was going wrong with their plan—and she was shooting him down as soon as he opened his mouth.

There was no way he could survive eighteen months of the silent treatment.

She swiveled in her seat and faced him. "Why does it matter? Did you ever talk to the hospital administrator?"

"Yes, as a matter of fact. He's thrilled for us."

She paled. "Are you serious?"

"I'm sorry. I don't know what is wrong with me."

He touched her arm. "And, yes, I'm serious. He wasn't upset. Just the opposite, actually. He'd like to feature us in some kind of promotion for Dia dos Namorados along with Adam and Natália, Marcos and Maggie, and some of the other married couples."

This time she laughed. Or it started out as a laugh, and swiftly changed to a weird keening sound that ended in a sniffle.

He put a finger under her chin, turning it toward him. "What's going on, Sara? Besides what happened the other night. Or is it because of that?"

"No, it's not about that at all. Well, it is, but not in the way you think."

"I have no idea what you're talking about."

"I'm talking about my dad."

His heart gave a painful thud. "Your dad? Is he okay?"

"He's fine. It's not his health I'm worried about." She closed her eyes for a moment. "He's coming to visit. Next Monday, in fact."

"What?" There was no way he could have imagined this happening. Or maybe he could have, if he hadn't been in such a damned hurry to screw up his life. And Sara's. No more drinking for him. Ever.

"Yes, and I haven't told him. About us. About the baby. I was going to wait until I was further along, but since I'm not in the nurses' dorm any more, he is certainly going to figure something out. Because I know good and well he's not going to expect me to be living under the same roof as you."

Her father probably wouldn't be thrilled that he'd taken his daughter to a motel right under his nose either.

"We'll figure something out." When he'd thought about things getting worse, never in a million years had he imagined them getting this much worse. Not only was

Antônio Moreira's daughter married, she'd married his oncologist, and she was now pregnant with that oncologist's baby. What a mess.

He started the truck, setting the air-conditioner to high as he tried to think through this thing logically. His lips twisted. An easy task, since everything about their marriage *reeked* of logic. He decided to be honest. "I'm coming up completely blank."

"I know. Me too. Barring asking you to move out of your own house, I have no idea how to fix this."

"Exactly how would me moving out solve anything?"

"I could say I was house sitting for a friend."

The muscles in his mouth jerked sideways in a smile. "Some friend, this friend."

"You know what I mean."

"And here I thought this was all about me."

Her head tilted. "What was?"

"I thought your irritation was because of what we did. Never mind. If you think my moving out temporarily will be the best solution, I'll do it."

"No. I was kidding." She smiled. "Okay, half kidding. But we were going to tell Daddy eventually. And someone at the hospital is bound to spill the beans. We'll just get it over with and do it when he gets here. We fell madly in love and decided to get married."

"In a matter of weeks. You think he's going to buy that?" Although maybe it was better to just throw it out there and see how he reacted.

"If I know my father, he'll probably be over the moon. That's part of why I didn't want to tell him right away. Well, making sure the pregnancy has time to take root was a big part of it, but I also don't want him to be hurt." She sighed. "He always wanted me to find the love of my life like he did. He's going to be so disappointed when he hears we're getting a divorce."

"He can't expect everyone to have the same kind of luck as he did." His parents certainly hadn't. And Sebastian didn't see himself having that kind of luck either. He already knew he didn't, if this was anything to go by. His parents had felt forced into marriage, kind of like he had. Only in trying to stick it out, they'd made themselves—and their children—pretty damned miserable. It looked like he really was a chip off the old block. His dad would be proud.

"I know. I just hate being the one to shatter his illusions. I've already disappointed him once, in that area."

He wasn't sure what she meant by that last sentence, and didn't feel like asking. "If what you said is true, he may be so happy to meet his grandchild that a lot of the extraneous stuff will fly out the window. Especially if we make sure that our split is as amicable as possible."

"I hope so." She took one of the pamphlets that advertised their clinic services and fanned herself with it. "Do you think we could start driving so that the air-conditioner works better? I'm about to be steamed in my own skin."

"Of course. Sorry."

"Don't be sorry. It's just a relief to not have you flip out about this."

"Why would I flip out?"

"Um. Because not only did your one-night stand get pregnant. And not only did you marry her to save her job and your pet project, but now her dad is coming to visit and expects to see his little girl put on a happy face."

"You want us to put on a good show for him, is that it?"

"I can't ask you to do that."

He pulled out of the parking lot and onto the busy street. "Of course you can. It won't be that hard. We both have to work this week, so the only time he'll see us is when we're home." He flashed a look at her. "Damn. When we're home. He'll have to stay with us, or he's going to know something is off, which means…"

She nodded her head and glanced sideways at him. "We're going to have to share a bed again. Only this time it will be completely chaste."

He waggled his eyebrows at her. "Not necessarily. Especially since your lip is doing its cute little puffer fish imitation."

"Oh, no. That was your last hurrah, mister."

"My very last one? Forever?"

She laughed, although it came out sounding a little choked. "Hasn't it gotten us into enough trouble?"

"Yes. It has." He popped his shoulder joint to relieve the ache building in it. "But it was at least a little fun, wasn't it?"

"Maybe a little."

He had to content himself with that, because the tone of her voice gave her away. It hadn't been a "little" anything. And Sebastian, Sara, and her lower lip all knew it.

Talita Moises met them at the door. "You were right. About everything. I'm having surgery to try to scrape that silicone junk out. Or at least try to fix things as much as possible. At the very worst they'll have to remove both of them. I wasn't sure how I felt about that, but there are worse things."

She'd taken a one-hundred-and-eighty-degree turn from where she'd been last week, when she'd said she didn't want to lose her breasts.

It was kind of hard to say "Congratulations" to a

woman who might be facing a double mastectomy. "How do you feel about that?"

"I should be sad, but I'm not. I'm just relieved it's not cancer. The doctor said my diabetes might cause some problems in healing, but he's hopeful. I won't know ahead of time whether I'll come out of surgery with boobs or without. The doctor said there was really no way to tell until he gets in there and sees how much damage has been done. I'll just be so glad not to have to deal with this any more that I don't really care what he has to do."

It was kind of surreal, hearing the change in Ms. Moises' attitude toward a possible mastectomy. Of course, Sara had changed her mind as well, hadn't she—going from swearing Sebastian to secrecy about her pregnancy and their marriage to agreeing to sleep in the same bed as him the whole time her dad was here? But only as a way to pretend that they were a happily married couple.

Pretend, Sara. You need to remember that!

Sebastian glanced her way. "Have they set a date for surgery yet?"

"The doc is squeezing me into his schedule, so it will happen in two weeks."

Right after Sara's father left to go home.

The woman clasped her hands together, picking at a piece of chipped red polish on her thumbnail.

"What's wrong?" She'd seemed happy enough a minute or two ago.

"I'm worried about where my grandson will go if something happens to me."

Sara laid her hand on the woman's shoulder. "Like I told you last time, nothing is going to happen to you."

It was dumb to promise something like that, she knew it, but somehow the words just came out of her mouth.

"It might. I'm no fool. And I don't have any relatives left."

"None?" A flash of pain went through her heart. She couldn't imagine being totally alone in this world. Sara had her father. And friends back home. And she would soon have a child.

But not even Talita was totally alone. She had her grandson. "How old is he again?"

"Twelve. He'll be thirteen in two months."

"Hmm, let me see what I can do."

Sebastian sent her a warning look. He was right. But she'd already blurted it out. It wasn't like she'd promised to adopt the boy or anything. And a mastectomy wasn't brain surgery, where the outcome wasn't certain. Not that any surgery was certain. But surely it wouldn't hurt to give the woman one less thing to worry about. If worse came to worst, maybe they could house the boy while his grandmother was in the hospital.

Somehow she didn't think Sebastian would like that. And there might even be a hospital rule against it. She would have to check. But, in the meantime, she could ask around and see if anyone would be willing to look after him for a week or so.

"Would you do that for me?"

There was such hope in her eyes that Sara couldn't bring herself to say no, even though she never should have said yes in the first place.

"I will. I'll see if I can find someone, and I'll let you know."

Talita grabbed her hand in both of her own. Tears ran down her cheeks. "Bless you. And thank you. You can't know how grateful I am."

She could know. It was written all over the seventy-eight-year-old grandmother's sweet face. And she didn't care if Sebastian was glaring daggers at her. He could go stay at a hotel if he didn't like it.

Although it would be the second time in a day that she'd asked him to do just that. But there had to be some kind of compromise that would work for everyone. The last thing she wanted was for a government agency to step in and take a boy away from an obviously loving home.

She and Sebastian would be sleeping in the same bed next Monday when her father came to visit. Why not extend that a little bit, since their patient's surgery would be in two weeks, right about the time her dad went back home. It couldn't hurt to ask.

Right. She had a feeling it was going to hurt at least a little once she left this house.

If not physically then emotionally, because Sebastian was probably going to let her have it with both barrels.

But what else could she do? If the patient didn't get the surgery she needed, she might die of infection at some point. And if she didn't feel secure in thinking her grandson would be well taken care of, then she might refuse to go through with it. No, Sebastian was going to agree to this. The same way that she'd agreed to this cockamamie marriage. And if he didn't, then she was going to make sure the next two weeks were some of the most miserable of his life.

CHAPTER EIGHT

THEY'D NEEDED THE BREAK.

At least that's what Sebastian had told her. She had an idea this was more for his benefit than for hers. But it didn't matter. She was going to be traveling to the top of a really tall building. Again.

But at least there hadn't been one of those freaky window-washer contraptions strapped to the outside of the Edifício de Banespa.

Evidently people were only allowed five minutes at the lookout area and then had to leave. Even so, there was a line of people waiting to go up in the elevator. A lot of them were couples or lovers. In fact, everywhere she looked there were people linking arms or caught up in their own world. Not her and Sebastian. After the busy day spent in the *favela,* she had gone home, showered and gone to sleep almost immediately. They had the day off today, so he'd suggested they come here.

He probably just didn't want to be home alone with her. And that was a good idea. Less chance of things taking a wrong turn. Again.

"Ten people, please." The elevator doors had opened and the guard was ushering sightseers into the elevator. He counted down until he reached Sebastian. "Ten. You're the last one, sir."

"We're together. I'll wait."

And it was true. They were together, but not by choice.

Except it had been, or she wouldn't be standing in a line with this man and wearing a gold band on her finger. Her thumb went to the back of it, sliding back and forth over the smooth surface.

The guard found a single person to take the last spot. Suddenly she envied that young man. He could just go up there and not worry about a partner. Or whether he regretted taking the leap that she had. One that was changing a lot more than just her name.

Her father was coming in less than a week, and they had a photo shoot to get through before that. "It could be worse," she muttered.

Sebastian tilted his head. "What could be worse?"

"Just thinking about the timing of the photo shoot. It would be worse if my dad were here, because he'd want to see us do it."

His mouth ratcheted up. "I don't think that's a requirement for marriage any more."

"Oh!" Her face flamed with heat. "I didn't mean that."

"I know what you meant." He paused, his smile fading. "Have you thought about how you want to break the news to him?"

"No, but I guess we should sit down and make some kind of plan."

"You're going to wait until he arrives?"

"I hadn't really thought about it. Do you think I should tell him before he gets here?" How big a shock would it be to arrive and find them sleeping in the same room? Probably a pretty big one. "Are you going to tell your parents?"

His lips tightened. "No."

"Not at all?" Shock and—yes, she could admit it—a

tinge of hurt came over her at the cold way he'd said the word. He'd mentioned his parents didn't have a happy marriage. Was he afraid that they would be upset over his choice? Or did he just not care what they thought?

"Not at all. They won't ever visit, so there's no reason to."

"And what about their grandchild? Will you keep that from them too?"

Just then the elevator opened and people from another group exited. "The next ten, please."

Saved by the bell. Or the elevator. They all piled in, the fit a little tighter than she expected it to be. She tried to shift her bag in front of her and ended up elbowing the man beside her in the stomach. He gave a sharp *"Mmph"*.

"So sorry," she murmured.

The doors closed with an ominous whoosh, and people jostled each other, trying to find an extra inch or two of space. Sara, on the other hand, stood stock still, too afraid to move.

A sense of claustrophobia prickled along her spine, sending shards of discomfort spiraling into her brain. It sent a message back: escape!

Only there was nowhere to run. *Deus.* Her heart rate sped up. What had she been thinking, letting him talk her in to coming here? They weren't even at the top and she was already a bundle of nerves.

She twisted around, needing to reassure herself that he was there, as steady and calm as always. She couldn't remember seeing him frazzled. Ever. Even when she'd told him she was pregnant, he hadn't gone off at the deep end and flipped out like she would have expected him to do.

There he was. That rock-solid body and deep brown eyes.

When his glance met hers he frowned, his head tilting in question. She was being ridiculous. But when she turned back to face the ticking numbers, an arm snaked around her waist, drawing her into his narrow circle, back from the crush of people. And just like that her heart slowed its frantic pace and the buzzing in her skull turned into the lull of background noise. She leaned her head back against his chest in relief, allowing the warmth of his body to seep through her. His arm tightened further, and she slid her hands over it, afraid he might let go.

A minute later the doors opened and people spilled out onto the concrete surface of the viewing area, all of them anxious to see as much as possible in the five minutes they were allotted.

"Thank you," she said in a soft voice as she pulled out of his embrace. "It was a little close in there."

His hand slid down to grip hers. "I thought you were about to ask me to boost you up to the hatch in the ceiling."

"There was an escape hatch? Now you tell me." She grinned up at him, startled when something dark went through his eyes. His fingers released their hold.

"I always make sure there's a way out."

Was he talking about elevators? Or relationships?

Had her ex-boyfriend done that same thing? Had his escape been planned the whole time?

It was probably better not to think about that. What if Sebastian decided he wanted no part of fatherhood after the baby was born? Or when he or she was five years old? Ghosting her as easily as her ex had. After all, São Paulo and Rio Grande do Sul were several states apart. How long before the traveling back and forth to see his child became a chore, and the visits ground to a halt? Or if he chose to remarry and start another family with someone else?

The thought had her struggling to catch her breath.

Before she could walk away, though, he reached for her hand again and gripped it tight, holding her in place.

"What?"

"If you thought my apartment was high, this is even higher. How close do you want to get to the edge?"

Okay, she had remembered that, and yet she hadn't. Her body relaxed, thankful to have something else to fix her thoughts on. "How many flights of stairs are there?"

"More than you want to think about."

"Great." She took a deep breath. "Okay, how close do *you* want to go?" As long as he was holding her hand, she would be fine, right?

"I want to go all the way to the edge and back, but I'm willing to restrain myself if that's not what you want."

A shiver went over her. Why did she keep hearing double meanings behind everything? Maybe because the low thrum of his voice always gave her crazy ideas. Or maybe it was simply because she was at the top of a building, where the air was impossibly thin. Did she trust him? If he pulled her all the way to the guard rail, was she going to have a meltdown?

No. The way he'd held her in the elevator had made her feel safe. Protected. Just like the way he was holding her hand right now. Just like when he'd made love to her. "I don't want you to hold back. Let's go together."

He threaded his fingers through hers. "Okay. Together."

They walked over to the guard rail, and her free hand clenched around it.

"Still okay?"

She hadn't quite trusted herself to look yet. "I think so."

"Here." He moved around behind her and wrapped his

arms around her middle, just like he had on the ride up. Her unease disappeared almost immediately.

"I love it up here," he murmured, his chin coming to rest on the top of her head.

She allowed her eyes to focus and...

Oh, boy.

The view was horrifying and beautiful all at once. As far as the eye could see, there were buildings upon buildings upon buildings.

The ranching town where she came from had apartment complexes, but nothing like these. Nothing like this gorgeous *vista*. She didn't look down. Instead, she kept her gaze pointed toward the horizon. "You said we could see Vista do Vale from here."

"Yes, the condo is..." His voice paused for a second. "Just off to our right."

She turned slightly to the right, but everything was one jumble of shapes that seemed to go on forever. "I don't see it."

"Let me see if I can show you." He shifted until his cheek was pressed tight to hers. "It's the cobalt and white building about ten blocks out and at your one o'clock. It's one of the tallest in the group."

She looked a little bit closer, using his instructions to narrow her search, except all she could concentrate on right now was the feel of his skin against hers. She started chanting inside her head: *Cobalt and white. Cobalt and white. Cobalt and...*

There, she could see it! "It looks so small from here."

His cheek scraped across hers as he nodded, the rough edge of his whiskers awakening nerve endings she'd rather remained dormant.

"Don't forget it's located in a valley and it's some distance away. Perspective can get skewed."

Yes, it could, because with him so close that his body seemed to enfold hers, she realized it would be far too easy to get used to this. To go from thinking of their marriage as a necessary evil to something that was comfortable and…exciting.

She breathed in deeply, his scent mixing with that of the city. São Paulo seemed to have soaked into his very pores. He was as grounded here as she was in Rio Grande do Sul.

She'd do well to remember that. She'd always known her move here wasn't meant to last forever. It was to help her learn ways to help people like her father.

Neither of them said anything for a few seconds as they continued to look out over the downtown area. She did her best to enjoy these moments and not think about the future.

"How much time do you think we have left?"

If he had said seventeen months and twenty days she wouldn't have been surprised, but he didn't. "Only around two minutes."

"It's all going by so fast." A flash of sorrow hit her right between the eyes as she realized she meant that in more ways than one. "Right now I just want to stay here forever."

The warmth of his breath made wisps of her hair flutter. "Everything comes to an end. Or it should."

The cynicism behind those words made her ache inside. "Not everything. Not life. Love. The birth of children."

"Even those things don't last forever."

"The cycle does, though, don't you think?"

"Yes. Some of them. But they're usually the ones you don't want to continue."

A small commotion on the other side of the viewing

area caught her attention. A huddle of people suddenly broke apart and a young man, maybe in his thirties, staggered out of their midst. His eyes were wide and terrified, face red. He slumped to the ground almost immediately. Someone screamed, "Daddy! What's wrong?" The words were in English and a tiny girl leaned over his chest, patting his face with chubby little hands.

Without a word, Sebastian released her and jogged toward the group, leaving her to hurry after him. Even before he got there, he was taking charge of the situation. He switched to English. "I'm a doctor. What has happened?"

A woman knelt down beside the girl, trying to pull her back, but it only caused her to wrench against the restraining hands and cry even harder. "I don't know! He just suddenly grabbed his throat as if he was trying to cough." The sheer panic in her voice was unmistakable.

Sebastian leaned over the man, putting his head to his chest. "Was he eating something?"

"Just this." The woman handed him a package that said "Soja Torrada"…toasted soybeans.

"Does he have allergies?"

"No. Not that I know of." Tears started pouring down her cheeks. "Can you help him?"

In an instant, Sara was at the man's head. Every second was critical. The man's breath wheezed in partially and then went silent. He'd stopped breathing.

The woman fell to her knees beside them, clutching the child to her chest. "Oh, God, someone do something!"

"Sara, tip his head to the side. I'm going to try something."

She did as he asked, instinctively turning him to face away from the mother and daughter.

Sebastian put one hand over the other, placing the base

of his palms on the man's abdomen just under his chest. Already the victim's face was turning dark as his circulation pumped unoxygenated blood through his system.

Thrusting his joined hands sharply toward the man's diaphragm, while Sara made sure his mouth was open, the first attempt yielded nothing. By this time there was a crowd around them. Even the man from the elevator was there, no longer counting the minutes. He repeated the attempt, then a third time, his compression even harder. Something flew from the man's mouth and landed on the ground a few inches away. A nut.

Sebastian had been right.

Hoping the man would start breathing on his own, alarm swept through her system when he lay lifeless on the concrete. No rise or fall of his chest, no improvement in his color. It had been less than a minute since he'd collapsed.

Sebastian put his fingers against the man's neck. "I have a pulse, but it's weak."

Working as a team, they straightened his head, the oncologist beginning mouth to mouth while Sara counted the puffs of air as they went in. When they reached seven, Sebastian paused and listened. Still nothing.

"Do you want me to take over?"

"Just count." With that, he went back to breathing for the victim.

Come on. You can do it!

She wasn't sure if she was willing the words to Sebastian or to the man on the ground.

"Seven."

Pausing again, he lifted his head.

This time there was a weak gasp, and then another. Suddenly the man took a huge gulping breath. After the third one, his eyes fluttered, but they didn't open.

His wife—if the ring on her finger was any indication—grabbed his hand. "Max! Can you hear me?"

Still a little blue around the mouth, he barely nodded, then his eyes opened, seeking the woman and child immediately. One arm reached toward them.

Relieved murmurs went up all around them. One person clapped and several others joined in. It was a little too soon to assume everything was going to be all right, though.

The man's mouth opened, but Sebastian stopped him with a quick shake of his head.

"Don't try to talk." He glanced up at the elevator attendant, who was standing a few feet away. "We need to take him down with as few people as possible. Can you have an ambulance waiting for us?"

"Yes, of course." The man walked a few steps away, speaking into a cellphone.

Sebastian turned toward the woman. "His name is Max?" His English was fluent and easy, while Sara struggled to keep up with the strange words.

"Yes. We're here on holiday." She gripped her husband's hand. "Is he going to be all right?"

When the child whimpered again, Sebastian reached over and tugged a lock of her blonde hair, giving her a reassuring smile. "He should be just fine. Don't worry, okay?"

The gesture made Sara's chest ache. Would he one day comfort their child like this? His words from a few minutes earlier came back to her, making the ache grow. Or would he walk away from them, thinking this was one of those cycles that should end?

He glanced at her. "I want just the family and us on that elevator. The fewer people the better."

"I'm...okay." The croaked words came from the man on the ground.

"You need to go to a hospital and get checked out. We work at one not far from here." He paused as if trying to gather his thoughts. "It's for the best."

"Max, you need to go," his wife said. "Please."

He gave a short nod, not trying to say anything else.

Already he had pinkened somewhat, but Sebastian was right. They needed to make sure he hadn't aspirated anything else. Even a tiny piece of food trapped in a person's lungs could cause inflammation or, worse, aspiration pneumonia.

The girl scrambled out of her mom's grip and landed on Max's chest, her small arms going around his neck. "Daddy. I love you!"

He returned her hug, his arms snug around her back, even though it was obvious his strength hadn't completely returned.

"Let's get you out of here. Do you think you can get up, if we help?"

Max glanced up at them and gave another nod. "Think so."

With Sara on one side and Sebastian on the other, they levered him up and slowly walked to the elevator, the crowd parting around them with more clapping.

She could only imagine the fear of being in another country and going through a crisis like this. Actually, she could imagine at least a little bit. Her own crisis wasn't life or death, but she was away from the only home she'd ever known, thrust into a strange city, and then discovered she was pregnant.

And what had been the result of all of that? Sebastian had attempted a metaphorical Heimlich maneuver, hoping to avert disaster for the program. Only unlike in

Max's case, where the rescue attempt had worked, Sebastian might have unwittingly thrown them into a situation that was far worse. They would find out when her father came to visit. A tough old cowboy, he had an uncanny ability to see through people as easily as he could judge a steer. He'd warned her about her boyfriend, but she hadn't listened, too infatuated with the idea of love to pay attention to the warning signs. Until it had been too late.

Would her dad realize that this was just an act?

He would be devastated, if so.

They got onto the elevator, and although he tried to wave off their help, Sara kept her shoulder wedged under Max's arm. Sebastian did the same while his wife stood in front of him, still holding his daughter in one arm. She touched his face, murmuring to him in soft tones. He nodded yes or no to whatever she was saying.

Behind Max's back, Sebastian's hand touched Sara's elbow. She leaned her head back slightly to look over at him.

"Thank you," he mouthed.

There was something in his expression that made her stomach cramp. She sent him a nod and a slight smile.

When they arrived at the ground floor and the doors opened, there was indeed an ambulance waiting. The emergency crew came forward with a gurney, while Sebastian filled them in on what had happened and what he thought the prognosis was. There wasn't enough space for all of them to ride, and the trip through São Paulo wouldn't be a walk in the park anyway because of the huge amount of traffic. But this was no longer a life or death situation, so Sebastian didn't need to ride with them. He did give Max's wife his card, telling her to call him if they needed anything while they were at the hospital.

As they loaded her husband in through the doors, she used her free arm to hug the oncologist, whispering something into his ear.

When the EMTs helped her and her child into the back of the ambulance, Sara came up to stand beside him. "What did she say?"

His jaw was tight, and he appeared to be battling some kind of raw emotion. "She said, 'You just saved my whole world.'"

Pinpricks needled the backs of Sara's eyes. "She loves him very much."

"So it seems."

She nudged him with her shoulder. "Still think everything comes to an end?"

"I'll have to get back to you on that."

The ambulance pulled away from the building and forced its way into the snarls of traffic, siren wailing and horn giving off long blasts of sound. Then they were swallowed up by the never-ending sea of vehicles. "They should be okay."

"Glad we went up?"

"Oh, yes. And very glad you didn't boost me up to that escape hatch. We were right where we were supposed to be."

He turned and looked at her, his expression unreadable. Then he leaned down and kissed her cheek. "Yes. We were."

CHAPTER NINE

SEVEN COUPLES WERE lined up outside the hospital, each of them awaiting their turn with the photographer. And Sebastian felt like the biggest kind of fraud. Every single one of these people thought their unions would last forever, judging from the arms casually slung around waists and subtle touches. His marriage, on the other hand, had an expiration date built right into it. Eighteen months. No more. No less.

He never in his wildest dreams imagined he would marry for the sake of a child.

Unlike his mom and dad, though, he refused to linger in a marriage built on the wrong motives. He'd told Sara the truth when they were at the top of the Banespa building. Oh, in the aftermath of that choking crisis yesterday, when Max's wife had murmured those heartfelt words to him, his world view had quaked in its foundations a time or two. But the old cynicism had returned.

Ha! But that sure hadn't stopped him from coming to this photo shoot and pretending to "love the one he was with". And Sara didn't look any happier about the arrangement. She was standing with her eyes focused on the ground, not even looking at the poses the first couple was given.

He couldn't blame her. There was mushiness right and left, along with a lot of gazing into each other's eyes.

What the hell had he been thinking, agreeing to any of this? He was not cut out to smile and pretend. He was… stoic. That was how he saw himself. None of the histrionics that had gone on in his childhood home. In fact, the quieter and more invisible he became, the better it was for everyone. Especially his sister, who had been fragile for most of her teenage years because of the cancer. He'd protected her from a lot of the drama. At least, he hoped he had.

Maybe that's why he'd been so quick to jump in and offer marriage to Sara. That protective instinct had never been totally snuffed out.

In fact, it was kicking in right now like it had yesterday, when they'd talked about escape hatches and when he'd held her out on that balcony. Pressed his cheek against hers.

It had all felt too good. Too real.

But it wasn't real. He needed to remember that.

He leaned down and whispered, "We can just leave, if you want." To hell with what the hospital administrator wanted. There could just be one less picture in their precious promotional article.

"It's already too late."

At least, that's what he thought she'd said. The words had been so soft, he couldn't be completely sure.

Too late for what?

"Are you feeling okay?"

She motioned him over to the side. "Remember when you asked me about my dad? And you asked if I was going to tell him before he got here? Well, I decided to go ahead. So I told him. About the baby. About us."

Okay, he wasn't sure what that meant. She'd told him the truth? Or she'd given him their cover story?

"He knows what, exactly?"

"Well, it would be kind of awkward for him to get here and say, 'Oh, by the way, I'm sharing a bed with the man who was your doctor.'"

Ah, okay, so that answered that. She'd told him that they were married.

"What was his reaction?"

Her head cocked to the side. "He was happy. Horribly, terribly happy."

The words "horribly" and "terribly" fit the situation. But to put them together with "happy"? That just seemed like an oxymoron. "In other words, he bought the story."

"That's what I just said."

Another couple was called to the forefront. Sebastian had no idea where they were in the queue.

"So that's a good thing, then. It should make his visit a piece of cake."

"No." She looked at him like he'd lost his marbles. "He is going to expect me to be like him and Mom. And— and—" Moisture rimmed her eyes, just like it had yesterday. Only this was for completely different reasons. And he'd caused it. All of it.

Damn! In trying to help her, he had made things infinitely worse. Which was why she'd said it was too late. It was done. And they were stuck.

Except that in eighteen months she was going to have to go through the explanations all over again. And he doubted her father would be quite as happy.

Unless they chose to stay married.

Um, no. Then he *would* be following in a set of footsteps that he despised.

"It'll be okay, Sara. We'll figure this out." He put his arm around her shoulders.

"Sebastian and Sara Texeira?" The call cut through the air like a knife and every head turned in their direction.

Hell, could this day get any worse?

He unhooked his arm from around her and linked their hands—to keep up the pretense. "Let's get this over with," he muttered, trying his best to plaster a pleasant expression on his face. It wasn't easy when every muscle in it felt stiff and frozen.

A second later, Sebastian was seated on a little stool with Sara standing behind him, her fingers curled like claws into his shoulders.

"Can I get a smile from the bride?" The photographer's mop of black hair flopped to the side as he peered out from behind his camera.

A few seconds later, a titter of nervous laughter came from those still in the area. Sebastian glanced up and over his shoulder to see what Sara was doing. Oh, Lord. Her lips were cranked skyward in the most unnatural expression he had ever seen. And that sexy bottom lip was nowhere to be seen.

The photographer got up and made his way toward them. "Okay, it's normal to be nervous. Maybe we'll try something without a smile."

"I'm sorry…" Sara started, only to have the man give her a wide grin that was much more spontaneous. A little too spontaneous, if you asked Sebastian.

Sebastian's frown grew when the photographer came up beside her, using cupped palms to tilt her head downward and to the right. "We'll just have you look at each other, how's that?" His hands kept fiddling with her pose, touching her arm here. Her waist there.

When he leaned a little too close, steam gathered in Sebastian's head.

Camera boy was beginning to really get under his skin. Did he know she was pregnant? Was he even an adult? He looked like a gangly kid from where he was sitting.

"Dr. Texeira, can you kind of peer over your shoulder at your wife?"

He did as he was asked, seeing the nerves still alive in Sara's face. He reached up and laid his hand over one of hers to reassure her.

"Yes, that's it. Hold it just like that."

Sebastian nodded at her and tightened his grip just a touch, feeling her relax, a lock of hair falling over her shoulder. With the sun behind her, she looked soft and radiant and—beautiful.

And there was that lip. Puckered just right.

At that second, he heard the tell-tale click of the camera. It went again and again, as they stared at each other.

Her eyes. Her upturned nose.

That sexy mouth.

"Okay." The sharp clap of the man's hands broke through whatever had been holding him in place, and he blinked.

Swallowed.

Sara took her hands off his shoulders and shoved the errant lock back over her shoulder.

"Let's try something a little different."

Sebastian frowned. "You mean we're not done?"

"I want just a couple more shots, and then I'll let you pick one to take home with you." He studied them for a second or two. "Why don't we have—Sara, wasn't it?"

When she nodded, he continued, "Sara, why don't you come and sit on your husband's lap."

"Excuse me?"

"Here." When the man acted like he was going to reach for her hips, Sebastian pre-empted him by gripping them and tugging sharply. She tumbled onto his lap, her arms going around his neck to keep from careening onto the ground.

Their cheeky photographer just laughed. "That's it. Just like that. Hold it."

Sebastian's right arm anchored her in place, while the man studied them from a couple of different angles. When she whispered, "I'm going to kill you," he just smiled.

"Better that than me killing that damned photographer." He kept his voice low enough so that only she heard him.

As if on cue, the guy was back, standing directly behind Sara, tilting her head back and resting it against his abdomen for a second. The muscles in Sebastian's neck went stiff with rage. This was no longer cheeky. It was unprofessional and inappropriate. When his gaze clashed with the photographer's the man's eyes widened slightly, and he took a step back. "That should do."

He took three more pictures, and Sebastian had to give it to the man. Inappropriate or not, he knew exactly how to play up Sara's features. With her head tilted back, the long line of her neck was on display. Her hair fell in a curtain that went past his hip, almost touching the ground. Her eyes were closed, probably from embarrassment, but to a casual observer it probably looked like she was waiting for his lips to slide over her throat. And if they had been alone, he would have been tempted to do just that. He would have bent over her and used his mouth to—

"Okay, that's it. Thank you."

Sebastian almost groaned aloud. Parts of him had

woken up unexpectedly, putting him in an awkward position. Sara's back came up as she straightened and her hip pressed hard against him. Air hissed through her lips, and she jerked around to stare at him. She'd felt his reaction.

Lord, how could she *not* feel it?

Her brown eyes crinkled at the edges.

"Can you get up?" Her voice shook slightly as if holding back laughter. Oh, she thought this was funny, did she?

"What do you think?"

"I think you already are." She popped off his lap, leaving him to somehow uncurl his body in a way that didn't reveal exactly what this little photo shoot had cost him. To his surprise, Sara stood in front of him, giving him a chance to collect his senses and put his life—or rather his body—back into some semblance of order.

"If you'll go over to the computer and take a look at the shots, while I get the next couple set up, that would be *bacana*. They're right on the monitor in the order they were taken. Just select the number beside the image you like best and write it on the card with your name."

They actually had to look at the photos? Great. But at least it gave him a chance to send blood flowing back into his head, rather than pooling in his groin.

They moved over to where the camera was set up. The shots were there, just like the man had said.

"Do you have a preference?"

When he glanced over, Sara was staring out at the landscape.

He chuckled. "You might actually have to look at the screen in order to choose."

"Ugh, I can't."

So he did it for her, and what he saw took his breath away. That stilted grin picture was there, but as soon as his eyes tracked to the first posed shot, he knew the photographer had done his job a little too well. The ones of her behind him showed a loving couple gazing deeply into each other's eyes. One right after the other, the angle of the camera lens changing just slightly between those three shots. When he came to the images of her on his lap, his throat tightened.

He'd thought she was beautiful when she was standing up? These pictures were magazine-worthy. Sebastian was staring down at her, his lips curved just slightly. And she looked totally lost in the moment, carefree and happy, one of her legs lifted off the ground to help her keep her balance. He remembered those long slender calves wrapped around his waist less than a week ago.

Damn. He wanted it. Wanted her. All over again.

"This one." He tapped the monitor.

As if fighting an inner battle, her eyes swung toward the screen. Her hand went to her throat. *"Misericórdia."*

Have mercy? It should have been him asking for mercy.

"Do you think your dad will believe it now?"

"*I* almost believe it." As if realizing what she'd said, she glanced quickly at him. "You're a very good actor."

He hadn't been acting. And in the shot he'd chosen—the very first of the lap pictures—he could still see a trace of the anger in his face over the photographer's hands being on her. He was almost in a swooping position, ready to protect what was his.

Only she wasn't.

And he'd better not start wishing she was, because he was the last person she needed. She deserved someone who actually believed in love and fairy tales. Who wasn't afraid to show emotions like anger and frustration. Who wouldn't always wonder if he'd married her for herself—

or because of what he'd done to her. Didn't they used to call that "doing the honorable thing"?

There was no honor in marrying for that reason.

Irritated at himself for even letting his thoughts wander in that direction, he scribbled the number down on the card. "I think we're both pretty good actors when we want to be. One more task to cross off the list."

He stood up, his body once more firmly under control, and he flipped the card onto the small stack of cards of the couples who were already finished with their photo shoot.

Well, so was he. He was finished. And *pelo amor de Deus*, he'd better damn well remember that.

They weren't the only ones who'd chosen that picture. The day her dad was to arrive, a huge publicity poster appeared in the entryway of the hospital. Perched on an easel, it proclaimed:

> *Hospital Santa Coração:*
> *A place where hearts are healed—*
> *and love is found.*

And the image at the very center of the poster was their lap dance.

Heavens, had Sebastian seen this yet? She hoped not, although how could he have missed it, as he'd been called in early to treat a patient? Maybe they'd just put the poster up.

The pictures of the other smiling couples surrounded them, but it seemed the photographer had put them all in much more conventional poses, reserving the most embarrassing one for her and Sebastian. The guy had made her feel a little uncomfortable, but even worse was Sebastian's reaction to it. For a brief second, she'd wondered if he was jealous. And then there was his...*reaction*. A very physical kind of reaction. It had nudged her as she'd moved to get up, shocking her. She'd had her eyes firmly closed to block out the experience, because she'd felt a familiar tingling awareness when she'd stood behind him and he'd looked up at her with those sexy hooded eyes she loved so much.

Loved?

No, not loved. She was only thinking that because of that huge, glaring word on the poster. It was sending a subliminal message, burrowing into her brain like a screwworm.

No matter. In the three hours since Sebastian had left the apartment, she'd gotten her things and moved them into his bedroom. Thank God his bed was huge—larger than any bed she had ever seen before. She could just put a stack of pillows between them and it would be as if they each had their own island to sleep on. She would simply get dressed in the bathroom in the very unsexy garb she had purchased for just this occasion. Not that they would be tempted to do anything with her dad practically sleeping in the next room. She was being ridiculous.

Shaking herself back to awareness, she wandered over to the elevators, trying to keep her head down and hoping no one recognized her as she headed to her appointment. Although she looked totally different in that picture than she did in real life. At least she hoped she didn't carry around that besotted expression everywhere she went.

They were supposed to pick her dad up at the airport at five this afternoon. Sara had tried to convince Sebastian to just let her go on her own, but he'd insisted, saying her father would think it was strange if she arrived by herself.

"He'll just think you're working."

His brows had edged up. "But I'm not."

"But you could be."

They'd gone back and forth a few more times before she'd slumped into a chair in the living room. They'd finally compromised. He could go with her to pick up her father, but he wasn't allowed to go to the prenatal exam he'd talked her into.

She took a deep breath. It was going to be okay. Her dad was only going to be here for a week. Sebastian wanted to do a little blood work on him and check his cancer markers. He didn't expect there to be any changes, but it didn't hurt to do a quick check. "Thank you. I owe you."

He'd given her a strange frown she still didn't understand. It was almost as if she'd said the wrong thing. But that didn't make any sense. It was a figment of her imagination. Much like their marriage.

Within seconds the elevators shuttled her to the correct floor, where Natália stood waiting for her. She swooped in for a quick hug.

"Hey, *moça linda*, how's married life treating you?"

God, she felt like such a liar. This was Sebastian's sister and one of her closest friends. "Oh, you know. We're still trying to figure things out, just like any other married couple."

"Okay, then," was all she said. Natália didn't believe her—and who could blame her? As someone who was also recently married she probably saw right through the sham. Or had Sebastian already told her it was all a farce?

"Are you sure it's not too soon to do this?"

"Nope. If you're eight weeks, we should be able to see something. Maybe even the heartbeat, if we're really lucky."

She nodded, following her down the hallway, doing

some quick calculations in her head. She'd been in São Paulo for... "Maybe a couple of days over eight weeks."

"I thought so. That was right about the time of my and Adam's wedding. I had no idea you and Sebastian even knew each other that well."

Squirming inside, all she could do was nod again. "We went out to get a few drinks after the wedding and things just...happened." No need to mention the reasons behind it.

"I know how it is. I have to admit I feel a little bit responsible. Sebastian wasn't himself once he found out about me and Adam. He was still acting out of sorts and moody at the wedding."

What was she trying to say? "We're both adults. He didn't take advantage of me, if that's what you're implying."

"Oh, God, no. Sebastian could be raging drunk and he would never lose control of himself."

That was funny, because Sara remembered them both being kind of out of control. Although Natália was right. She couldn't really recall many times when he'd totally lost it. Hmm. The night they'd had sex in his bedroom *could* be considered one of those times. And then when the pictures were being taken. And— It didn't matter. It was what it was. There was no wishing that things were different. They weren't and they never would be. He'd made that perfectly clear.

And Sara was fine with that. She had to be.

She decided to change the subject. "Can you do the ultrasound yourself?"

"I can. It might be better if you and an OBGYN do it, but I should be able to find something. We'll take a traditional pregnancy test as a back-up, just in case."

Ten minutes after Sara had peed into a cup, she found

herself lying on a table, ultrasound wand gliding across her belly. "Let's just see if we can find little Billy."

Sara rolled her eyes, trying to act nonchalant about the whole thing. "How do you know it's not a girl?"

"I don't. Billy can be a girl or a boy's name." The wand hit a ticklish spot, making her squirm. It then went back over the same spot.

"Are you doing that on purpose?" She choked out a laugh. "Let's change places and see how well you like it."

The second the words were out of her mouth, her laughter died a hard death. "I'm sorry. I didn't mean that."

There was silence for a couple of beats, then her friend smiled. "It's okay. I came to terms with the fact that I can't have children a long time ago. Actually, we're thinking of adopting at some point."

"That's wonderful." She shifted on the table.

"Let's try the left side." When Natália changed her location, she went "Bingo" within seconds. "There, do you see?"

Her friend pointed at a small blob on the screen, then fiddled with something, moving the transponder again. "Oh, Sara, look."

"Is something wrong?" Had she found some kind of horrible deformity?

"Nothing is wrong. Your baby's heart is beating."

She stared at the monitor, straining to find what the neonatologist was talking about. Then she saw it. A tiny quick movement. Rhythmic. Continuous.

A heart.

Her own swelled, and she was afraid to look away for fear that little flutter on the screen would suddenly stop. "Is it okay?" she whispered.

"As far as I can tell, everything is perfect. You need to have a real examination, though."

"I will." She swallowed, suddenly overwhelmed. "Okay, I've seen enough. Thank you."

Natália switched the machine off and the screen went dark. She had to bite her lips not to ask her to find the baby again. It was okay.

There really was a baby in there.

Her friend wiped the gel off her abdomen and pulled the gown back down.

"Thank you." She hesitated. "Could you come up here, please, if you're all done?"

"Sure thing." She moved to stand by her shoulder. "Do you feel better now?"

"Yes, a little. Can I sit up?" When Natália nodded, Sara jammed herself upright. "I can't believe I'm really pregnant."

"You really are, according to your body. But, then, you already knew that, didn't you? It's why you got married."

She put her legs over the side of the exam table, her hands clasped in her lap. "He told you."

Rather than continuing to stand, Natália hopped on the table beside her. "He didn't have much of a choice. I was all over him about marrying so quickly."

"He was trying to protect his project, and actually protect me too. He thought maybe they would remove me from the team if they thought there was any kind of impropriety."

"Instead you ended up getting roped into the Dia dos Namorados campaign."

She examined her toenail polish to keep from having to look directly at her friend. "That was a hoot, let me tell you."

"I bet. I saw the poster downstairs. If I didn't know better, I would think you two were in love."

"The photographer somehow pulled stuff out of his hat that wasn't there. Some kind of airbrushing trick."

"With your skin, I would be very surprised if he had to do anything."

A scoffing sound came up from her depths. "I barely even know him, Natália."

"You're carrying his child."

"Last time I heard, you didn't have to know anyone at all to carry a child. There are lots of ways to get pregnant."

"Yes, there are. And yet you looked pretty darned happy to see that baby's heart beating."

"I was. I'm not sure why. I should be frantic. Or horrified." And yet she was none of those things. She hadn't had time to sit and think about it. Until right now when she'd seen living proof that a baby was growing inside her.

The only thing that horrified her was the thought of her dad figuring out that her marriage wasn't built on love but on convenience and self-interest. They'd taken the picture from the campaign and had it framed, putting it on the mantel like they'd talked about. Just something to reassure her dad that she was okay. That she *would* be okay.

And she would be, no matter what happened between her and Sebastian.

"I think my brother is a lucky man."

Shock rippled across her nerve endings. "We're not going to stay together, Natália."

"You don't know that for sure." Her friend gave her hand a squeeze.

"I do know. We set a date to divorce after the baby is born."

"Well, that's interesting." If Natália was surprised,

she didn't let on. She just hopped off the table with an enigmatic smile. "Just remember. Plans change. So do people, if you give them some time."

Sara sighed and then got dressed before following the neonatologist to the door. Once there, she stopped for just a second or two and then gave a sad shrug. "Not these plans, Nata. And not these people."

CHAPTER TEN

SHE'D PUT A bunch of damned pillows down the center of the bed. Under the covers so they formed some kind of blockade.

Against what? Him?

Did she really think he couldn't just roll right over them and land on her side?

"This is more than ridiculous. You know that, right?"

Her muffled voice came from the far side of the mattress where she lay teetering on the edge. "I just didn't want to accidentally move to your side and crowd you."

"Crowd me. On a king-sized bed." Even he could hear the irony dripping from his voice. He was lying just on the other side of the barrier, but even if he stretched his arm as far as it could go, he wouldn't be able to reach her. And that was probably the point. But she couldn't stay there all night. In those long flannel pajamas in the dead of summer.

Her father's flight had been delayed twice before finally landing at almost midnight. They hadn't had much time to talk. Used to rising at the crack of dawn, the older man had dozed most of the car ride back to the condo. Once there, he was tired enough that he'd kissed his daughter and shaken Sebastian's hand with muttered congratulations.

The man hadn't asked a single question. About any of it. But he had no doubt that those would come tomorrow. Especially since they were scheduled to do blood work and a quick health check. And then he and Sara were supposed to head over to Tres Corações to meet with Talita, whose surgery had been moved up by a week. Natália and Adam had agreed to take care of Jorge until his grandmother got out of the hospital. Thank God, because he didn't think he would be able to survive having Jorge and Sara's dad here at the same time.

"I move around a lot in my sleep."

Yes, he knew she did. He'd slept with her before.

And yet as much as he was ridiculing her, he had to admit she was all kinds of adorable with her dark hair flowing across the white of his sheets. He laid an arm across the mountain of pillows. Nope, couldn't reach her. But he could tease her. At least a little.

"I had to turn the air-conditioner way up. I don't normally wear this many clothes to bed." Actually, he didn't normally wear any. The pajama bottoms were for her benefit. He didn't think she would appreciate him coming to bed naked, even if she had seen him that way before.

She gave a weird cough. "It is kind of warm tonight, although Daddy thought it was chilly in the apartment. He doesn't use anything but fans at home. It's taken a little getting used to for me as well. The hospital I worked at before I came here had air-conditioning, but it was broken most of the time."

He propped his hands behind his head. "It sounds like you loved your life there."

"I did." She rolled over to look at him. "I always loved watching my dad rope steers. He always seemed so— strong, you know?"

He really didn't, since his dad had never been someone he'd looked up to. "He's still a strong man."

"It scared me, seeing where he was a year ago when
the cancer caused him to break his leg. I thought he was
ready to give up."

"But he didn't."

"Thanks to you and Natália." She scooted closer to
the barricade and leaned up on her elbow, her long hair
just touching the mattress. Now he could reach her, if he
wanted to. He forced himself to stay where he was, content to hear the sound of her voice.

It was almost—normal. Was this what some couples
did every night?

"It was all Natália. She was the miracle worker in this
case. Her surgery was similar enough that it made your
dad think he might have a good outcome as well."

"And he did."

"Yes, he did."

She fiddled with the fabric on one of the center pillows. "I appreciate everything you've done for us. His
surgery. My position here at the hospital."

He didn't like where this conversation was headed.
The last thing he wanted from her was her gratitude. It
made him wonder things like whether she'd slept with
him the night of the wedding because she'd been trying
to pay a debt.

No, she wasn't like that. And since she was a nurse,
it was unlikely that she'd been indulging in a little bit of
hero-worship. He'd never encouraged that with patients,
and he knew the boundaries that needed to be set and
kept. So what had happened with Sara?

He'd gotten good and drunk. And she'd been so beautiful, carrying an air of vulnerability that he hadn't understood. Still didn't, in all honesty. But beneath all of that

lay a heat and fire he hadn't expected. It had consumed him that night. Burnt him alive.

The ashes were still glowing, waiting for the slightest breeze to tease them back to life. Even those silly chaste pajamas couldn't extinguish it. Or her attempt at a pillow levy bank.

Right on cue, something in his body stirred.

He moved, so that only the bridge of pillows was between them. "The program needed you. I needed you."

It was true. In more ways than one.

"And I needed it." She gave a heavy sigh, plumping the pillow beneath her hands. "The opportunity came at just the perfect time."

He could barely see her over that damned mountain she'd created.

"Don't you think this is idiotic? We're expecting a child together."

"It just seems kind of funny with my dad in the same house." She lifted her head a little higher to peer over the pillows at him.

"He's not right next door. And the rooms in this place are pretty damned soundproof. He couldn't hear you if you screamed the place down."

She blinked at him. "Why would I do that?"

"Guess." Parts of him lifted higher than ever. "I know exactly what you sound like."

"Sebastian!" Her voice was a shocked whisper.

"He can't hear you. But if you prefer to play it safe…"

All of a sudden he didn't want safe. He wanted dangerous. And forbidden. And the woman lying less than a foot away was even more beautiful than when he'd first laid eyes on her.

"Play it safe?"

Did he hear a glimmer of disappointment? All he

knew was that he wanted to go down this road just a little further. Tease her just a little bit more.

He reached under the covers and plucked one of the pillows, sending it sailing over the side of the bed. The first brick in her flimsy little fortress—gone. "Safe—as in if we're very, very quiet, your dad won't hear us at all."

She squeezed the pillow she held tighter. "I don't remember either of us being all that quiet."

Parts of him were now pulsing, demanding he listen.

"I'm always up for a challenge." He reached over and took the pillow from her and tossed it behind him, putting them face to face. "How quiet can you be? I bet I can come without making a single sound."

Her loud gasp made him chuckle. "Oh, not good. You're already failing the first part of the experiment."

Reaching out, his fingers encircled her wrist and tugged her onto the pillows, flipping her on her back. "But I can think of a very, very good use for these. And it has nothing to do with keeping us apart and everything to do with bringing us together."

With that his head came down, and he found her mouth, taking it in a kiss that seared his own senses, even as she squirmed to get closer.

He wanted her. Father or no father. The fact that she was carrying his child made it even sweeter.

Fingers swiftly parted the buttons on her pajama top and his lips moved to the first of the pink nipples he'd uncovered. Sucking it hard, he relished the way her back arched as she pushed toward him. The tiny moan she gave turned him to molten lava, making him release his hold to look down at her. "Shh. I need this. And I think you do too."

Straddling her hips, he gathered her wrists in one hand and carried them over her head. "You do, don't you?"

He whispered the words against her lips. "Need this as much as I do?"

She gave a single nod. "But please be quiet."

"I will." He stretched out on top of her and parted her legs, pressing himself hard against the heart of her, "I guarantee it. But I can gag you, if you're worried about yourself."

Sara bit her lip when he ground against her again. Then she leaned up and kissed the side of his mouth. "I won't be the one making any sounds."

"It's too late. You already did."

The back and forth whispering was intimate. Sexy. And his body was aching for her. Mouth against her ear, he slid slightly to the side, leaving just enough room for one hand to skate down her still-flat tummy and edge beneath the elastic of her bottoms. He went past her panties, and curved around until he was just where he wanted. She was hot. Wet. And he'd done almost nothing except talk.

Well, he was all done talking. Sitting up, he stripped her of her bottoms, laying her bare to his gaze.

Deus! He didn't ever remember being this hot for a woman.

His fingers moved up to her face, then captured a strand of her hair. He drew the blunt end down her nose and across her lips, which parted. His erection twitched and strained.

"Time to make good use of these pillows." He stacked them three high, while she watched. "Now. Come here, Sara."

As soon as she got on her knees, he took her pajama top and slid it down her arms before moving behind her. His fingers trailed down her spine, curving up under arms and cupping her breasts. "So perfect." He squeezed the nipples, leaning down to bite the side of her neck.

She gave a tiny whimper, not much louder than their whispered talk had been. But it was enough to tell him it was time.

"Lie over the pillows, baby." He put a hand between her shoulder blades and applied slight pressure. She obliged, her body aligning perfectly so that her hips were elevated, while her torso lay flat on the mattress. His hands squeezed those perfect ass cheeks, before moving up to grip her hips, one hand going down to release himself.

Taking a second to position himself, he found that moist heat he'd discovered earlier.

Bracing himself, he thrust home, burying himself inside her silky flesh.

That tiny whimper came again. He leaned over, pressing his front to her back and scooting his hands underneath her. One at that tight puckered nipple and the other at the nub of flesh at the V of her legs. He flicked both, pulling his hips back and then plunging forward once again. Her breath rasped in and out as he repeated the act. He couldn't hold it together much longer. Not any longer, in fact.

Changing tack, he gripped her nipple between his thumb and forefinger and began a rhythmic squeeze that matched his thrusts. He buried his lips in the hair at her nape as her whimpers grew more frantic. "I love the way you squeeze me. Like this." He tightened his fingers around her in both places, still pumping hard and fast. And just like that she fell apart around him, her body convulsing as she buried her face in the mattress and made all kinds of sexy muffled sounds. Unable to stop himself, he plunged deep and let the ecstasy take hold, pouring everything he had into her, teeth gripping the soft skin of her neck.

He was done. Completely done.

Satiated, he lay there and took stock of the situation. He heard no movement from any part of the apartment. No sense that they'd been discovered. Sara's back was soft and supple, her muscles completely relaxed.

Maybe he wasn't so done after all.

They could have fun with this. A whole lot of fun.

He pulled out, smiling as she gave a breathed protest. He licked the spot on her neck that he'd just bitten. "Don't worry. We're not finished." With that, he flipped her onto her back, hips still elevated by the pillows. "But let's try it this way this time."

With that, he lifted her to his mouth and watched as he got ready to ravish her all over again.

She loved him.

Sitting across from him at the breakfast table, she felt the same trill of fear she'd felt last night as she'd listened to him sleep. Those deep easy breaths that had spelled total contentment. How was she going to give him up in eighteen months?

Maybe she didn't have to. He couldn't have made love like that without feeling something for her, right?

"Do you want some eggs, Daddy?" She held a plate out toward her father.

Sebastian had seemed distracted this morning. Oh, he talked easily enough with her dad, but it was almost clinical. He asked questions about his health as if he were any other patient.

And she'd caught her father glancing between her and Sebastian with open speculation in his eyes.

Surely he couldn't have guessed.

"Everything looks great, honey." He took the bowl and served himself a healthy portion. It made her smile.

Breakfast had always been important in their house. Her dad worked long hours and claimed he needed food and plenty of it to sustain him throughout the day. In reality, Sara thought he did it because it made her mom so happy to cook for him.

A pang went through her heart. What would her mom think of her daughter's deceit?

She would be so disappointed. She was a firm believer in telling the truth whenever possible. Everything about Sebastian and her relationship had been built on a lie. From that time in the motel, when they'd both had too much to drink and she'd been looking for a way to ease her heartache, to their marriage, to those pictures and beyond.

Only what she'd felt for that lost boyfriend paled in comparison to how Sebastian made her feel.

Unbidden her eyes went to the mantel where that photo was on display. A sense of nausea slid up from nowhere, gripping her stomach and squeezing tight. She took a bite of toast.

"Everything okay, sweetheart?" Sebastian's voice carried a question. Only it too was a lie. Sweetheart? She wasn't his sweetheart. Maybe she would never be.

She forced a smile. "Fine." She took another tiny bite, hoping the dryness of the bread would soak up whatever pool of acid was forming in her belly. She swallowed. Then gulped again when it did nothing but add to her troubles.

"I'll tell you the truth. I was mighty surprised to hear that you two had gotten married. Especially since Sara's last boyfriend was a big city man as well. Although I think that one knows better than to ever show his face at the ranch again."

"Dad!" She was horrified that he was even talking about this right now.

"What? I'm just glad to see that there are still some good men out there. And I'm sure you got married for the right reasons."

Her eyes shot to Sebastian's, who laid down his fork a little too carefully. "I think it was."

She almost snorted. Of course he thought it was. He'd been saving his project.

"Love shows up when you least expect it, though, isn't that right?" her dad went on.

This time Sebastian didn't even attempt to answer. Didn't attempt to even pretend that their marriage was based on that particular emotion. Her heart squeezed so tight she could barely breathe.

She needed to stop this. Now.

"Daddy, I think you're embarrassing him."

Her husband's eyes met hers. Cool and indifferent. As if last night had never happened. "Not at all."

"Sorry if I'm speaking too plainly. She's my only child. I want to make sure she's happy."

Happy. Now, there was a fickle word. And what a difference twelve hours could make.

"I understand."

"Adding a baby so soon will add some stress, but I know you two can work through it." Her dad smiled at her. "Your mom wanted more children, but you were it for us."

Why was he saying this? Her hand went to her belly in a protective gesture.

Sebastian saw it, his gaze hardening slightly. "Lots of people only have one child."

"Yes, they do. But it was the one thing that Dalia wanted that I couldn't give her. Even after thirty years of marriage, it was still hard for her to accept. I would have sold my soul to give it to her."

"Oh, Daddy, she loved you for you."

"I wasn't perfect. I think sometimes she just stayed with me because of you."

An odd sound came from the other side of the table. She glanced over to see that Sebastian's jaw was rigid, white lines forming on either side of his mouth.

"That's not true." She said it in a rush, trying to circumvent a disaster in the making. She remembered Sebastian talking about his parents and how they had stayed married for the sake of the children. "You two loved each other very much."

"Yes, you're right, of course." He forked up a bite of eggs and chewed for a minute or two, looking at her with a frown. "I'm sorry, this has nothing to do with your relationship. I know you'll have a long, happy marriage just like your mom and I did."

Her husband picked up his fork again and stabbed at a piece of ham on his plate. He said nothing. Didn't try to reassure her father, didn't try to reassure her. Because there was nothing he could say without tossing one more lie onto an already stinking pile.

If anything, he seemed to be studiously trying to avoid looking at either of them.

In that moment, Sara realized it was hopeless. They were not going to have a long, happy marriage. Because he didn't love her. It was never going to happen. She was pretty sure her dad might even realize that. He'd hurled those barbs like little jokes, but they'd caught at Sebastian's throat and given him a bad case of laryngitis. Maybe it was better that he didn't try to defend his actions.

Her nausea increased fourfold and her gaze returned

to that picture. How carefree she'd looked in it with her head thrown back and her husband smiling down at her as if he—as if he loved her.

Only he didn't. He'd as much as admitted it.

Her eyes pricked with tears. She'd been living in a fantasy world. Oh, not at first. She'd sworn she could handle this fake marriage and all it entailed. Sebastian had sure been able to.

Her dad had it all wrong. They'd married for the worst of reasons. It hadn't even been about the baby. It had been trying to save both of their asses from the possible consequences of their actions. Consequences that might not have even come to pass. They should have just confessed and let the chips fall where they may.

And now she'd committed the ultimate sin. She'd fallen in love with the man.

And in seventeen months—if they even made it that long—he would walk away from her without a second glance. Just like her ex had.

"Hey, you two." Her dad was looking from her to Sebastian. "Did I commit some kind of faux pas? I'm not really acquainted with the rules in the big city."

Sebastian laid his fork down once again. "Of course you didn't. I just have a big case I'm working on that has taken all my energy. In fact, if you'll excuse me, I need to get to the hospital."

"Of course." Her dad stood to his feet. "I think Sara was going to take me to see some tall building that she says will give me a great view of the city."

"The Edifício do Banespa." Her husband's glance landed on her, before skipping away. "Yes, it has a great view."

A great view. He could have been talking about any normal building. There was no mention of how he'd held her tight against him during that long elevator ride. Or how he'd pressed his face close to hers as they'd looked for this very building.

Who was she kidding? He *was* talking about just another building. Because that was all it was to him.

She had to close her eyes for a moment to fight to keep the contents of her stomach inside her. Seventeen months?

There was no way. She wouldn't last that long.

Sebastian would guess the truth long before then. Hadn't he realized how scared she'd been on that trip to the top? He would realize she loved him in a month, if not sooner.

And it would drive him away long before she was ready.

What choice did she have?

She could leave.

She could wait a week or so after her father left and then she would follow him—tell him that she realized she really had married Sebastian for the wrong reasons. He would be devastated, but he would get over it. Just like she would.

She followed them to the door, plastering a fake smile on her face that resembled the macabre grin she'd had in the first picture of the photo shoot. But nothing she tried made it look any more natural.

Because nothing about this situation was natural.

Sebastian would make a great father, and there was no way she would keep him from his child, despite her words in his office all those weeks ago.

Wow, had it only been weeks?

At the entrance, Sebastian leaned over and kissed her on the cheek, but the light touch seared like the branding iron her dad used on his steers, and she jerked away from it.

"See you when I get home," he said.

"Sounds good. Drive safely." The words had a sour taste as they came out of her mouth.

Oh, God, how was she going to sleep in that bed again after all they'd done in it?

She didn't know, but she'd better figure it out. Or else she needed to confess the truth to her dad and get out long before then.

Maybe even before Sebastian came home from work.

He closed the door behind him without a backward glance.

Yes. She and her father could just leave. Go to the Banespa building. Look at the city, and then over lunch she'd lay it all out.

She could raise a child alone. People did it all the time. And she was positive there were plenty of people who loved someone who didn't love them back. This was her second time around that particular block.

Knowing it didn't make it any easier, though.

Her dad glanced over, his smile fading in a hurry. He wrapped his arm around her waist. "Sara, what is it?"

"Oh, Daddy…" Turning, she buried her face in his familiar shoulder and burst into tears. Between sobs, she said, "I've made the biggest mistake of my life. I got pregnant. And he doesn't love me. He never has, and we just did this to save my job and his project, and it was never supposed to be real, but now it is. And I don't know what to do."

He didn't try to put a stop to the incoherent babbling or tell her to back up and start again. He just held her as she poured her heart out to him in a long stream-of-consciousness torrent. When she finally wound down, he took hold of her shoulders and held her away from him, studying her face.

"You love him."

"Yes, but didn't you hear me? He doesn't love me back. And he won't stay with me once this marriage runs its course." She didn't go into Sebastian's parents or how he hated that they'd stayed together in a loveless, bitter union. And that's what their marriage would turn into as well: a dry empty husk. Oh, the sex might keep him coming back for a little while, but it wasn't enough to build a real relationship.

And did she really want a man to stay with her just for the pleasure he found in her body? Bile washed up her throat all over again.

No, that was not what she wanted. And that was not what she would settle for.

So, is this the end?

Yes, it was. And she'd better get used to it, because like Sebastian had said up at the top of the Banespa building.

Everything eventually came to an end.

Even their marriage.

CHAPTER ELEVEN

"ARE YOU SURE this place is safe?"

Sebastian had a new nurse.

And no wife.

"We'll be fine. The people we're treating aren't hit men." Irritation bubbled up in his throat, most of it directed at himself.

A month after coming home to an empty house, he still couldn't believe Sara had just walked away without saying a word. And when he'd tried to call her, Antônio had answered and bluntly told him not to call back until he figured it out.

Figured what out? He had no idea what the hell he'd even done wrong.

Really?

His behavior at the breakfast table had been atrocious, but he hadn't been able to stand listening to Mr. Moreira talk about how wonderful his marriage was and watch Sara sink further and further into herself. It was all Sebastian's fault. He'd practically shoved this marriage idea down her throat and forced her to go along with it. Had basically threatened her with losing her job if she didn't.

What kind of person did that?

His father, that's who. A man who lied and cheated

and went to motels to have cheap sex with women he didn't love.

Sebastian had done exactly the same thing. And he'd compounded it by lying and cheating to get what he wanted: the Mãos Abertas project.

He'd gotten it. And lost his self-respect in the process. And a friend.

A friend?

Hell, he had no idea what Sara was to him.

It didn't matter in the end, because she was gone. He'd simply told Paulo Celeste that she'd gone home to help her father for a while. He hadn't elaborated any further than that. And surprisingly the man hadn't asked questions, he'd simply assigned him another nurse. Another punch to the gut. He could have avoided all of this.

And his baby?

That was still a huge unknown. Sara had told him he could be a part of the baby's life as long as he was sure he could be there for the long haul. Well, she must have changed her mind about that. There'd been no word on how either of them were doing.

Don't call back until you figure it out.

"What's the woman's name again?"

"It's right there in the chart." He fired the words at her and immediately regretted his attitude. It wasn't her fault he'd screwed up his life. He took one breath. Then another. "Sorry. Her name is Talita, and her grandson's name is Jorge."

He turned down the narrow street that led to her house, finding the crude board fence with ease. Maybe he needed to do something about that. Surely he could spend a few hours fixing up some things around her house. And it would give him something to think about besides his sorry state.

"Someone actually lives here?"

Something about the nurse's words made his hackles rise all over again. It wasn't all her fault. Santa Coração dealt with wealthy patients for the most part. This was a foreign world to many of them—to most of the staff as well. Besides Marcos and Lucas, there weren't many people who had actually spent a large amount of time in a *favela*.

Well, if she wanted to work with him, she'd better get used to it and fast. "Yes, someone does. Do you have a problem with that?"

His grouchy attitude was back with a vengeance.

"No. Of course not."

Well, at least he'd knocked a bit of the haughtiness from her voice.

He turned off the truck and got out. This was more of a courtesy call than anything. Talita had had a double mastectomy three weeks ago. She'd healed well, and the doctors told her she shouldn't have any more episodes of lipogranuloma.

She was still working on her blood sugar, which was why they were here.

At least, that's what Sebastian told himself.

"Do you want me to bring her chart?"

"Sure. Why not."

Veronica Cantor's mouth thinned, but she didn't say anything else as they arrived at the entrance and Sebastian clapped three times.

Within seconds, the door was thrown open by Jorge, who held his fist out for a teenage version of a handshake. Sebastian bumped his own against it with a smile. "How have you been?"

Jorge looked past him at the Mãos Abertas truck, probably looking for Sara. He hadn't said anything to Talita about the break-up, and he was swiftly realizing that coming here might not have been the best idea.

"Who is it?" The grandmother's voice came from inside the house.

"It's Dr. Sebastian and some..." Jorge looked the nurse up and down and Sebastian got ready to give him hell if he said what he thought the kid was thinking of saying. But to his credit, the boy filled in the blank with the word "lady".

"Well, don't just keep them standing outside in the heat."

Jorge ushered them in, not that it was much cooler in the house. But a fan in the living room at least moved the air around enough to take his mind off the oppressive humidity.

Talita, seated on her customary floral chair, glanced at Veronica and then at him. "Where's Sara?"

"She went home." Those simple words came out of his mouth before he could catch them.

He wasn't here to check up on her. He was here to— He had no idea.

Don't call back until you figure it out.

Talita motioned her grandson over. "Why don't you take Nurse...?" She sent Sebastian a glance.

"Her name is Veronica Cantor."

The older woman nodded. "Take Ms. Cantor to see the game system Sara sent for your birthday."

Sara had sent him something? Hell, Sebastian hadn't even known it was the kid's birthday.

How did she do that? Make everyone feel special?

Until they were no longer on her radar.

Veronica shot him a glance, and he nodded at her. Talita was either going to lecture him or console him.

He didn't need to be consoled.

He just wanted to be left alone.

Ha! Wasn't that what Sara had done? Left him alone?

Dammit, maybe he shouldn't have come here after all.

As soon as Veronica and Jorge had left the room, Talita waved a hand at the ragged faux leather sofa next to her chair. Suppressing a roll of his eyes, he lowered himself onto it, but decided to go on the offensive. "How are you feeling?"

"I'm fine. How are *you* feeling?"

She'd turned it around on him, the emphasis on the penultimate word making Sebastian laugh. "Are we really going to do this?"

"Do what?" The older lady batted her sparse lashes at him.

"What do you want me to say? Sara decided she wanted to go home. So she went."

She and her father had slipped out before he'd even gotten home from work. The day after they'd made love.

Don't call until you figure it out.

That phrase had been knocking around in his head ever since that phone call.

"Why did she decide to leave?"

"I don't know."

Talita stared at him long enough to make him wince, her lips twisted in thought. "I wondered why the postmark on Jorge's present said Rio Grande do Sul. Is that where she's from?"

He nodded, not sure where she was going with this. "Her dad is a *gaúcho*."

"When is she coming back?"

This was one question he knew the answer to. "She's not."

Antônio hadn't said it when he'd called, but the intimation was plain enough.

"I'm sorry."

"Me too." It was true. He was damned sorry. And he had no idea why. It should make his life a whole lot easier.

Maybe he didn't want easier.

She was gone, so it didn't really matter what he wanted.

"Did you tell her you love her?"

"No, of course not, I—" Too late he remembered Talita didn't know the real reason he'd married Sara: so that people like Talita could get the surgery they needed.

Only the project hadn't been sunk the moment she'd left. It may not have been sunk even without marriage. Although it still could have caught up with him.

Could have?

It had. Sara had left.

He kept coming back to that. Why did it matter that she was gone?

Talita gave him a sharp look. "You didn't think you loved her, did you?"

He shook his head, not even bothering to answer.

"But you do."

His brain caught on the words. No, he didn't. He couldn't.

It was impossible, because...

There was a gaping hole where that missing word should be.

A thunderbolt struck him in the chest.

He did. He loved her.

Which was why he couldn't seem to get past the fact that she'd left him high and dry.

Don't call until you figure it out.

Was this what he was supposed to figure out? That he loved her?

"Yes. I do." He shrugged. "But I guess she didn't feel the same way."

"She married you, didn't she?"

"Yes, but only because she felt she had to."

Which was the very reason he'd been so hung up over this whole thing. Why he'd set an end date. Because he hadn't believed that a marriage built on that premise—on a pregnancy—could last.

He still wasn't sure it could. His parents' marriage had, if you could call that miserable existence something that "lasted".

Talita leaned over and looked him in the eye. "Are you that blind? The last time I saw you two, it was written all over her face. The way that girl looked at you said it all."

He frowned. "The way she what?"

"She looked at you the way my Henri used to look at me."

"How did he look at you?"

A dreamy look passed across her face. "As if I was his whole world."

His throat clogged. Wasn't that what the woman at the top of the Banespa building had said?

You just saved my whole world.

He fought for something to say that wouldn't sound cheesy or patronizing. Or hopeless. He settled for simple. "How long were you married?"

"Twenty-five years. One child. And one grandchild."

Five years less than Antônio Moreira had been married.

Had Talita really read something in Sara's expression that had led her to believe she loved him?

And if she did?

Could he actually be happy with someone—with her—for thirty, forty or however many years they lived?

Yes. He thought he could.

He and Sara were not like his parents. He couldn't remember even one serious argument—oh, there'd been little ones, but not about things that mattered. They'd laughed together, worked together—made love together.

Veronica poked her head around the corner. "Can I come out yet?"

"No!" Talita and Sebastian both said the word at the same time. The older woman giggled like a girl when the nurse retreated back into the bedroom.

"So what are you going to do?" she asked.

"Her father told me not to bother calling until I figured something out."

She leaned closer. "I think you just did."

"I think you're right."

"He's probably wondering what took you so long." She crossed the stub of her left leg over her right. "So I'm going to ask again. What are you going to do?"

"I'm going to go down there?" Why he made a question out of it, he had no idea.

"You're damn right you are. And don't come back until she believes you, you hear? No matter how many times you have to say it."

He leaned over and kissed her cheek. "I hear you, Talita. Loud and clear."

Sara slid her hands into matching oven mitts and opened the door to the stove. The casserole inside sizzled. *Escondidinho*—one of her favorite dishes. It should be making her mouth water, and although the meat pie topped with puréed manioc smelled delicious, all she felt was a rock where her stomach should be.

It had been that way ever since she'd come home.

Because she'd run away from a difficult situation without saying a word to anyone. How was that any different from what her ex had done to her? It wasn't. But it was too late to go back and fix it.

Her father had been supportive and wonderful about everything, but over the past month she'd caught him staring out the window. When she asked him what he was doing, he said, "Nothing. Just thinking."

Probably wondering how he was going to survive toddlerhood all over again.

No, her dad said he was looking forward to having little feet running all over the place, and she believed him.

Clap! Clap! Clap!

Ugh! Not again! It seemed every time she turned around, one of her father's employees came over from the bunkhouse to ask some question or other.

It wasn't like her dad not to be out working the ranch. He still had to be careful with his leg, but two weeks ago he'd gotten a tentative okay to start riding a horse. At a walk. But he'd seemed more interested in that stupid window.

Was he worried that the cancer had come back? They hadn't had the chance to do the blood work Sebastian wanted.

She took off the oven mitts to answer the door, but her father beat her to it. Good, whoever it was could get the answer right from the source. She turned around to finish her lunch preparations, even though her stomach was still doing somersaults inside her. Just another month until her morning sickness should be over.

If that was even what this was.

The door clicked open.

"What in the hell took you so long?"

Sara's brows shot up as she took another step toward

the kitchen. She'd never heard her dad greet anyone that way before.

"It took me a while to figure it out."

She stopped dead in her tracks.

Deus. She was having some kind of stress flashback. That voice wasn't real. It couldn't be. Her guilt was making her hear things.

"And have you?"

Okay, that was her father's voice. It was okay. Just her imagination. She started to walk again.

"Yes. I have."

No. It wasn't her mind playing tricks. She swung around toward the door, but her father was blocking the view.

"Daddy?" she called out.

He glanced back and smiled. "There's someone here who wants to talk to you."

Her hand went to her throat. "Is—? Is it—?"

A man stepped around her father's form. "I hope it's *my* name you're searching for."

Sebastian. It was really him.

"What are you—? Why are you here?"

Her dad gave her a strange knowing smile. "Is that any way to talk to your husband? I think you should at least invite him in for lunch."

Lunch? *Lunch?*

She was having some kind of breakdown, and he was worried about missing a meal? He was acting like he'd been expecting Sebastian for ages.

The image of him looking out the window day after day came to her. Was this why? He'd expected Sebastian to appear?

Her dad swept past her, giving her arm a quick squeeze.

"Hear him out, okay? He's traveled a long way to see you. And to say it."

To say what? That he wanted a divorce?

Deus, that's what it was. He figured if she was no longer working at the hospital, there was no reason to keep up the pretense. She should have expected this.

What she hadn't expected was for him to come in person. He could have simply sent the paperwork by certified mail or something.

Once her dad was gone—listening from the kitchen, no doubt—Sebastian closed the door then slowly made his way over to her as if—as if he wasn't sure.

This Sebastian was different from the one who knew what he wanted and went after it. Or maybe she was still trapped in that hazy dream state from when she'd heard his voice at the door.

But he was here. This was a flesh and blood man. Her dad had seen him, had spoken with him, so he was real.

She lifted her chin. Okay, then. It was time to face him and get this over with. "Did you bring the papers?"

He nodded.

Her mouth popped open to help her force air into her suddenly aching lungs. "If you have a pen, I'll sign them and you can be on your way."

He rolled his shoulder in a way that made it pop. Her eyes burned. It had been forever since she'd heard that sound—since she'd heard his voice.

"Maybe we're talking about two different sets of papers." He pulled a sheaf of documents from a long white envelope, then his eyes came up and met hers. "I want to get married. Again. In a church."

Pain ripped through her chest. So soon?

"To who?"

One side of his mouth tilted up. "Do you have to ask?"

She guessed she did, or she wouldn't have voiced the question. But he was smiling. That sexy heart-stopping twist of lips that made her insides go all gooey.

It hit her. There was only one person he would be saying that about. She hoped.

She took her index finger and curved her hand around until it pointed back at herself, her eyebrows raised to make it a question.

"Yes, Sara. You."

"You want to marry me? Why? I thought you were coming to ask for a divorce."

"I don't want a divorce."

"You don't. Is it because of Mãos Abertas?"

He set the papers down on a nearby table. "It has nothing to do with the project. It has everything to do with you."

"The pregnancy, is that it?"

Why did she keep firing questions back at him as if unable to believe his request could be related to something besides all the obvious choices? Because the only other option was…

Surely not.

"This isn't about the baby. Or the project. Not this time. This is about you. And me. I want you to come home."

Home. As if that was where she belonged.

He reached for her hands. "I love you."

"No, you don't."

His head tilted. "I think I would know."

She tried to tug free, only to have his grip on her tighten.

"Please, stop. I already told you I wouldn't keep the baby from you."

"I love you. I'm going to keep on saying it until it sinks into that pretty head of yours."

"Did my dad put you up to this?"

"No, but when I tried to call you the day after you left, he told me not to call again until I figured it out." He lifted one of her hands to his lips and kissed it. "So I didn't call. I came instead. I love you."

Maybe he was really going to keep saying it.

"Are you sure?"

"I wouldn't be here if I wasn't." He nodded at the side table. "I brought proof. Unless you don't feel the same way about me."

"I did." She blinked a time or two to clear her vision. "I mean, I do, but are you sure you really want this?"

"I'm more sure of this than I've ever been of anything." He reeled her in until she was flush against him. "Marry me."

"But what about not being able to see a relationship lasting for decades?"

"I'm out to prove myself wrong. And you're going to help me do it." His fingers sifted through the hair at her nape. "Because I already know the outcome. We're going to last for the duration."

Muscles in her body that had been tensed relaxed against him. "That could be a very long time."

"I'm counting on it." He smiled. "And on having a few more babies along the way."

"More babies?"

"Does that scare you?"

"No. It makes me happy." She believed him. Her arms went around his neck and she raised her face for his kiss.

It was the same sweet fire she remembered, and it injected warmth to her very core.

"I want a real wedding. To make a real commitment.

Not because of any baby or babies, but because I want you to be my wife. My forever wife." He took her hand where her wedding ring was and slid it off her finger. At her shocked gasp he hushed her with a kiss. "Don't worry, I'll put it back on. At a ceremony, which will happen here at the ranch, because this is where it all started."

Their mouths met again. Clung. The promise of a lifetime full of love and happiness shimmered around them.

He pulled back, his lips still touching hers. "Do you think your dad would be shocked if we shared your bedroom tonight?"

"I doubt it, but that's not what I want."

When he made to take a step back she did what he had done earlier and tightened her grip. "I have something very different in mind."

"You do?"

"Mmm." She stood on tiptoe, rubbing her cheek across his. "Yes, because you said it all started here at the ranch. Well, that's where you're wrong."

"I don't understand."

"Think about it, Sebastian. Our relationship did not start here. And I want to spend the night in the place where it all began."

He stood there for a second and then his brows slowly went up.

"I see you're beginning to get the picture," she said.

"You want to spend the night at the—"

"Shh. We have to be very, very quiet." She knew he would get the reference to their shared night.

He lowered his voice to a whisper. "You want to start this new phase of our relationship in a sleazy motel? Remember, we now have a baby in tow."

"And I think our baby would say, 'Thank you very

much,' don't you? Since that's where he or she got their start."

He chuckled, biting her lower lip and sending a sharp pang of need through her belly that spiraled lower and lower.

"Do I think so? Oh, I do, Sara. I do indeed."

EPILOGUE

Baby Silas Texeira came on a stormy day.

But the one thing that wasn't stormy was Sebastian's heart. As the sound of thunder rumbled just outside the hospital, he leaned his head against his wife's, relishing her tired sigh as she whispered, "Love you."

"I love you." He kissed her cheek, his hand going to their baby's tiny back. "And I love our life."

He did. His heart gave a couple of hard beats. He'd worried so much about his motivation for staying that he'd realized he'd lost his way for a little while, almost never getting the opportunity to feel the joy that came with discovering a person in tiny bites. Those moments in time that were meant to be savored and enjoyed.

Yes, he'd jumped into marriage for the wrong reasons. But he was staying for all the right ones.

"Can I call them in?"

"Yes. Please do." She tried to drag her hands through her hair, but he stopped her.

"You look beautiful."

"No, I don't. But no one will be looking at me, anyway." She laid her hand on top of his. "He's amazing, isn't he? This little creature came from both of us."

He grinned. "Maybe we'll leave out some of the details of how he came to be, though."

"I want to go back to that motel every anniversary."

"Sorry?"

"We belong together. I want it branded on our souls, etched in our minds. The motel will just make the process fun."

"Little pitchers." He pretended to cover Silas's ears. "And I don't think it's appropriate to try to seduce me in front of a newborn."

She smiled back at him. "*Try* to seduce you?"

"Okay, so that's pretty much a done deal." He wanted her. All the time. Not because of the sex, although that had been pretty damned amazing. But because of Sara herself. She touched a part of him that no one had ever reached. And he couldn't get enough of her. Her ex-boyfriend had done Sebastian a huge favor in leaving, although if the man ever came back, he was probably going to meet the wrong end of Antônio Moreira's branding iron.

He kissed that cute lower lip. "I think we'd better let some people in here before the room starts to steam up."

She nodded, sighing as she gazed down at their child. "I guess we can share him."

"We might be facing a mob scene if we don't." He moved his lips to her cheek before forcing himself to stand up. "I'll go get them."

He ducked into the hall, and fifteen heads turned toward him in bright expectation. Marcos and Maggie, Lucas and Sophia, Sara's dad, of course. His sister and Adam.

Then his chest tightened. Because a little off to the side was Talita Moises in her wheelchair. Jorge stood directly behind her.

Talita, who had read Sebastian the Riot Act and brought him to his senses. Her blood sugar was finally under control once again. It looked like she would be there for the rest of Jorge's childhood and into his adult years as well.

He was just getting ready to ask everyone to follow him when one of the nurses from the front desk came barreling toward them. "You are not going to take all of these people in there at once, are you, Dr. Texeira."

Funny how that hadn't been a question but a statement. This particular nurse was known to be ruthlessly protective when it came to her patients. He could understand that. He was pretty protective of Sara as well. But this would be good for her.

He wasn't above a little bargaining to get his way. Unlike his dad, though, this was for a good cause. "How about if I take them all in, but we stay half the amount of time. They'll be in and out." He did a quick head count. "I think since most of us work at this hospital, we know how important it is for patients to get their rest. And since I'm her *husband*..."

For a second, he thought she might veto even that bargaining chip, but although her lips tightened, she gave a brusque nod and glanced at her watch. "Half the time would put you at five minutes."

"Five minutes sounds perfect." He led them down the hall and opened the door. While the rest of the group went in, he waited until Talita and her grandson wheeled up next to him. Laying his hand on her arm, he lowered his voice. "Thank you. For everything."

"I could say the same for you. If it wasn't for Mãos Abertas, I might not be here. How can I ever repay you?"

"You already did. Just by doing us the honor of being here."

"That girl is your whole world, isn't she?"

"Yes, Talita, she is."

"I knew it." She leaned up and pressed her lips to his cheek. "Don't be a stranger, okay?"

"Never."

Then she and Jorge went in to join the rest of the people who were busy oohing and ahhing over the baby and Sara.

As he stared at the gathering, a burst of gratitude sizzled inside him. He was a lucky, lucky man.

He went to the head of the bed and draped his arm on the pillow above Sara's head, watching as she laughed at something Natália had said. He was rich beyond his wildest dreams and it had nothing to do with money.

"Two minutes," he said, feeling a little like the elevator man at the Banespa building.

The nurse was right, though. Sara might look perfectly content, but she was exhausted from giving birth.

Besides, he wasn't quite as willing to share her and Silas as he'd thought. These moments were precious. Irreplaceable.

"Sebastian." His wife's voice carried a chiding tone he knew all too well.

"Nurse's orders."

Natália stepped forward and kissed Sara's forehead. "He's right. We shouldn't tire you out." She gave a pseudo-whisper. "We'll come back when your bodyguard is at work."

"I work here." Sebastian's dry response wasn't lost on anyone. They laughed, but all followed his sister's lead and congratulated them and filed out one by one. Talita and Jorge lingered a moment longer.

"You have a beautiful baby there, honey."

"Thank you." Sara squeezed the older lady's hand. "I hear you're the reason I still have a husband."

"Oh, he would have realized he was being a fool eventually. He just needed a big kick in the behind to understand it sooner rather than later."

"Can I call you whenever he needs another kick?"

"No need," said Sebastian. "I have learned my lesson."

Talita smiled and put her arm around her grandson's waist. "You have to come and eat at our house, once you're out of the hospital."

"Nothing would make us happier, right, Sebastian?"

"Absolutely."

Jorge smiled. Always quiet, he nodded toward the baby. "I could show him how to do things someday. Like maybe ride a bike."

Sebastian had probably heard Jorge say maybe ten words the whole time he'd known him. And the thought of this shy, retiring boy being willing to come out of his shell in order to help Silas made something in his throat grab. He coughed, trying to rid himself of the sensation. Then he put a hand on the boy's shoulder. "Silas would be very fortunate to have a mentor like you."

"Like a real mentor?" The boy stood straighter.

"Yes. Like a real mentor. He'll need one. So you'll have to set a good example."

Talita reached up to ruffle the teen's hair. "Oh, he will. And now we'd better be on our way." With a last flurry of hugs, Jorge wheeled his grandmother from the room, leaving Sebastian and Sara alone with their baby.

He kicked off his shoes and then settled into a nearby chair, propping his feet on the bed.

"You've been awake as long as I have. You need to go home and get some rest."

He reached for her free hand and gripped it tight. "I don't need to go anywhere, *querida*. If you're here and the baby is here, this is my home."

* * * * *

*If you missed the previous story in
the* HOT BRAZILIAN DOCS! *miniseries
look out for*

THE DOCTOR'S FORBIDDEN TEMPTATION

*And if you enjoyed this story,
check out these other
great reads from Tina Beckett*

RAFAEL'S ONE-NIGHT BOMBSHELL

THE NURSE'S CHRISTMAS GIFT

*TO PLAY WITH FIRE
(*HOT BRAZILIAN DOCS! *Book 1)*

*THE DANGERS OF DATING DR CARVALHO
(*HOT BRAZILIAN DOCS! *Book 2)*

All available now!

MILLS & BOON®
Hardback – September 2017

ROMANCE

The Tycoon's Outrageous Proposal	Miranda Lee
Cipriani's Innocent Captive	Cathy Williams
Claiming His One-Night Baby	Michelle Smart
At the Ruthless Billionaire's Command	Carole Mortimer
Engaged for Her Enemy's Heir	Kate Hewitt
His Drakon Runaway Bride	Tara Pammi
The Throne He Must Take	Chantelle Shaw
The Italian's Virgin Acquisition	Michelle Conder
A Proposal from the Crown Prince	Jessica Gilmore
Sarah and the Secret Sheikh	Michelle Douglas
Conveniently Engaged to the Boss	Ellie Darkins
Her New York Billionaire	Andrea Bolter
The Doctor's Forbidden Temptation	Tina Beckett
From Passion to Pregnancy	Tina Beckett
The Midwife's Longed-For Baby	Caroline Anderson
One Night That Changed Her Life	Emily Forbes
The Prince's Cinderella Bride	Amalie Berlin
Bride for the Single Dad	Jennifer Taylor
A Family for the Billionaire	Dani Wade
Taking Home the Tycoon	Catherine Mann

MILLS & BOON®
Large Print – September 2017

ROMANCE

The Sheikh's Bought Wife	Sharon Kendrick
The Innocent's Shameful Secret	Sara Craven
The Magnate's Tempestuous Marriage	Miranda Lee
The Forced Bride of Alazar	Kate Hewitt
Bound by the Sultan's Baby	Carol Marinelli
Blackmailed Down the Aisle	Louise Fuller
Di Marcello's Secret Son	Rachael Thomas
Conveniently Wed to the Greek	Kandy Shepherd
His Shy Cinderella	Kate Hardy
Falling for the Rebel Princess	Ellie Darkins
Claimed by the Wealthy Magnate	Nina Milne

HISTORICAL

The Secret Marriage Pact	Georgie Lee
A Warriner to Protect Her	Virginia Heath
Claiming His Defiant Miss	Bronwyn Scott
Rumours at Court (Rumors at Court)	Blythe Gifford
The Duke's Unexpected Bride	Lara Temple

MEDICAL

Their Secret Royal Baby	Carol Marinelli
Her Hot Highland Doc	Annie O'Neil
His Pregnant Royal Bride	Amy Ruttan
Baby Surprise for the Doctor Prince	Robin Gianna
Resisting Her Army Doc Rival	Sue MacKay
A Month to Marry the Midwife	Fiona McArthur

MILLS & BOON®
Hardback – October 2017

ROMANCE

Claimed for the Leonelli Legacy	Lynne Graham
The Italian's Pregnant Prisoner	Maisey Yates
Buying His Bride of Convenience	Michelle Smart
The Tycoon's Marriage Deal	Melanie Milburne
Undone by the Billionaire Duke	Caitlin Crews
His Majesty's Temporary Bride	Annie West
Bound by the Millionaire's Ring	Dani Collins
The Virgin's Shock Baby	Heidi Rice
Whisked Away by Her Sicilian Boss	Rebecca Winters
The Sheikh's Pregnant Bride	Jessica Gilmore
A Proposal from the Italian Count	Lucy Gordon
Claiming His Secret Royal Heir	Nina Milne
Sleigh Ride with the Single Dad	Alison Roberts
A Firefighter in Her Stocking	Janice Lynn
A Christmas Miracle	Amy Andrews
Reunited with Her Surgeon Prince	Marion Lennox
Falling for Her Fake Fiancé	Sue MacKay
The Family She's Longed For	Lucy Clark
Billionaire Boss, Holiday Baby	Janice Maynard
Billionaire's Baby Bind	Katherine Garbera

MILLS & BOON®
Large Print – October 2017

ROMANCE

Sold for the Greek's Heir	Lynne Graham
The Prince's Captive Virgin	Maisey Yates
The Secret Sanchez Heir	Cathy Williams
The Prince's Nine-Month Scandal	Caitlin Crews
Her Sinful Secret	Jane Porter
The Drakon Baby Bargain	Tara Pammi
Xenakis's Convenient Bride	Dani Collins
Her Pregnancy Bombshell	Liz Fielding
Married for His Secret Heir	Jennifer Faye
Behind the Billionaire's Guarded Heart	Leah Ashton
A Marriage Worth Saving	Therese Beharrie

HISTORICAL

The Debutante's Daring Proposal	Annie Burrows
The Convenient Felstone Marriage	Jenni Fletcher
An Unexpected Countess	Laurie Benson
Claiming His Highland Bride	Terri Brisbin
Marrying the Rebellious Miss	Bronwyn Scott

MEDICAL

Their One Night Baby	Carol Marinelli
Forbidden to the Playboy Surgeon	Fiona Lowe
A Mother to Make a Family	Emily Forbes
The Nurse's Baby Secret	Janice Lynn
The Boss Who Stole Her Heart	Jennifer Taylor
Reunited by Their Pregnancy Surprise	Louisa Heaton

MILLS & BOON®

Why shop at millsandboon.co.uk?

Each year, thousands of romance readers find their perfect read at millsandboon.co.uk. That's because we're passionate about bringing you the very best romantic fiction. Here are some of the advantages of shopping at www.millsandboon.co.uk:

* **Get new books first**—you'll be able to buy your favourite books one month before they hit the shops

* **Get exclusive discounts**—you'll also be able to buy our specially created monthly collections, with up to 50% off the RRP

* **Find your favourite authors**—latest news, interviews and new releases for all your favourite authors and series on our website, plus ideas for what to try next

* **Join in**—once you've bought your favourite books, don't forget to register with us to rate, review and join in the discussions

Visit **www.millsandboon.co.uk**
for all this and more today!